Henry Hucks Gibbs

The Romance of the Cheuelere Assigne

Henry Hucks Gibbs

The Romance of the Cheuelere Assigne

ISBN/EAN: 9783337008826

Printed in Europe, USA, Canada, Australia, Japan

Cover: Foto ©Andreas Hilbeck / pixelio.de

More available books at **www.hansebooks.com**

Early English Text Society.

Extra Series, VI.

The Romance

of the

Chevelere Assigne.

—

RE-EDITED FROM

THE UNIQUE MANUSCRIPT IN THE BRITISH MUSEUM,

WITH A PREFACE, NOTES, AND GLOSSARIAL INDEX,

BY

HENRY H. GIBBS, ESQ., M.A.

OF EXETER COLLEGE, OXFORD.

September 1897. For this year the Original-Series Texts were issued in 1894, and those for 1898 in 1896. The first for 1899 is now ready. The Extra-Series Texts for 1896 and the first for 1897 are also now ready. The texts of several other works are now printed. **Members are askt to send their two- or three-years' subscriptions for both Series at once in advance.**

The Original-Series Texts for 1896 are both dialectal : No. 106, Richard Misyn's—he was Prior of Lincoln—englishings in 1434 and 1435 of Richard Rolle of Hampole's *Fire of Love* and *Mending of Life*, edited by the Rev. Rt. Harvey, M.A., Headmaster of the Cork Grammar School ;—this Text, tho not in a pure dialect, is interesting for forms like *sarif*, for *serve*, &c.;—and No. 107, *The English Conquest of Ireland*, 1166-85, two parallel-texts of about 1425 and 1440, of which the earlier has now and then *dyng*, *tynge*, for *thing*, &c., edited by Dr. Furnivall.

The Extra-Series Texts for 1896 are from casts of books first issued by other bodies,—LXIX, Lydgate's *Assembly of Gods*, edited by Dr. Oscar L. Triggs for the University of Chicago ; and LXX, *The Digby Plays*, edited by Dr. Furnivall for the New Shakspere Society. As both these works form necessary parts of the E. E. T. Soc.'s Lydgate and Old-Play Series, and the Society was allowed to have casts of them for the cost of the plates, it took advantage of the opportunity to save money for other MS. texts.

For 1897, the Original-Series Texts are, No. 108, *Child-Marriages and -Divorces, Troth-plights, Adulteries, Affiliations, Libels, Miscellanea, Clandestine Marriages*, Depositions in Trials in the Bishop's Court, Chester, A.D. 1561-6, with *Entries from the Chester Mayors' Books*, 1558-1600, ed. Dr. F. J. Furnivall,—a most curious volume, full of the social life of its time ;—and Part II of the *Prymer or Lay-Folks' Prayer-book*, edited by Mr. Henry Littlehales, with a Paper by Mr. Bishop on the Origin and Growth of the Prymer.

For 1897, the Extra-Series Texts are LXXI, *The Towneley Plays*, re-edited from the unique MS. by Mr. George England, with sidenotes and Introduction by Alfred W. Pollard, M.A. ; and LXXII, Hoccleve's *Regement of Princes*, A.D. 1411-12, re-edited from the MSS. by Dr. Furnivall. The latter forms Part III of Hoccleve's Works. Part II will be Hoccleve's *Minor Poems II*, from the Ashburnham MS., edited by Mr. Israel Gollancz, M.A.; and if it is ready in 1897, it will be issued as LXXIII for that year.

The Original-Series Texts for 1898 are Nos. 110, 111,—Part II, Sections 1 and 2, of Dr. T. Miller's *Collations of Four MSS. of the Old-English Version of Bede's Ecclesiastical History*.

The Extra-Series Texts for 1898 will doubtless be the Second Part of the prose Romance *Melusine*—Introduction, with ten facsimiles of the best woodblocks of the old foreign black-letter editions, Glossary, &c., by A. K. Donald, B.A. ; and a new edition of the famous Early-English Dictionary (English and Latin), *Promptorium Parvulorum*, from the Winchester MS., ab. 1440 A.D.: in this, the Editor, the Rev. A. L. Mayhew, M.A., will follow and print his MS. not only in its arrangement of nouns first, and verbs second, under every letter of the Alphabet, but also in its giving of the flexions of the words. The Society's edition will thus be the first modern one that really represents its original, a point on which Mr. Mayhew's insistance will meet with the sympathy of all our Members.

The Original-Series Texts for 1899 will be No. 112, *Merlin*, Part IV, Prof. W. E. Mead's *Outlines of the Legend of Merlin*, with Glossary, &c., and No. 113, *Queen Elizabeth's Englishings of Boethius de Consolatione*, Plutarch's *De Curiositate*, and part of Horace, *De Arte Poetica*, edited from the unique MS. (a portion in the Queen's own hand) in the Public Record Office, London, by the late Miss C. Pemberton, with a Facsimile, and a note on the Queen's use of *i* for long *e*. The first Original-Series Text for 1900 will be No. 114, *Jacob's Well*, a quaint allegorical treatise on the cleansing and building-up of Man's Conscience, edited from the unique MS. in Salisbury Cathedral, by Dr. J. W. Brandeis.

The Extra-Series Texts for 1899 will probably be Miss Morrill's edition of the *Speculum Guidonis* in the Society's Guy-of-Warwick Series ; Mr. I. Gollancz's re-edition of two Alliterative Poems, *Winner and Waster*, &c., ab. 1360, just issued for the Roxburghe Club ; Dr. Norman Moore's re-edition of *The Book of the Foundation of St. Bartholomew's Hospital, London*, from the unique MS. ab. 1425, which gives an account of the Founder, Rahere, and the miraculous cures wrought at the Hospital ; or *The Craft of Nombrynge*, with other of the earliest english Treatises on Arithmetic, edited by R. Steele, B.A., or *Alexander Scott's Poems*, 1568, from the unique Edinburgh MS., ed. A. K. Donald, B.A.

An urgent appeal is hereby made to Members to increase the list of Subscribers to the E. E. Text Society. It is nothing less than a scandal that the Hellenic Society should have nearly 1000 members, while the Early English Text Society has only about 300 !

1 The first issue of the Glossary has been canceld, and a revised one issued.

The Original-Series Texts for 1901 and 1902 will be chosen from books already at press : Part IV (the last) of Prof. Skeat's edition of Aelfric's *Metrical Lives of Saints ;* Part II of the *Minor Poems of the Vernon MS.,* edited by Dr. F. J. Furnivall ; Mr. Gollancz's re-edited *Exeter-Book*—Anglo-Saxon Poems from the unique MS. in Exeter Cathedral— Part II ; Dr. Bruce's Introduction to *The English Conquest of Ireland,* Part II ; Dr. Furnivall's edition of the *Lichfield Gilds,* which is all printed, and waits only for the Introduction, that Prof. E. C. K. Gonner has kindly undertaken to write for the book. Miss Mary Bateson has at press George Ashby's *Active Policy of a Prince,* &c., from the unique MS., A.D. 1463. Dr. G. Herzfeld's re-edition of the Anglo-Saxon *Martyrology* is all in type. Part II of Dr. Holthausen's *Vices and Virtues* needs only its Glossary.

The Texts for the Extra Series in 1900 and 1901 will be chosen from *The Three Kings' Sons,* Part II, the Introduction &c. by Dr. Leon Kellner ; Part II of *The Chester Plays,* re-edited from the MSS., with a full collation of the formerly missing Devonshire MS., by Mr. G. England and Dr. Matthews ; the Parallel-Text of the only two MSS. of the *Owl and Nightingale,* edited by Mr. G. F. H. Sykes (at press) ; Robert of Brunne's *Handlyng Synne,* edited by Dr. Furnivall ; Deguilleville's *Pilgrimage of the Life of Man,* three prose versions —two English, one French—edited by G. N. Currie, M.A. Mr. Steele has also in type, besides the earliest Treatise on *Arithmetic,* englisht from Johannes de Sacro Bosco, two prose englishings of the *Secreta Secretorum* from MSS. at Lambeth, the second of which is very rich in new words. A version by James Yonge in 1428, made for the Earl of Ormonde, has been copied from its Rawlinson MS. at Oxford, and collated with the later Lambeth MS. All three versions differ widely. Some of these Texts will be ready in 1897. **Members are therefore askt to send Advance Subscriptions for 1898, 1899 and 1900,** in order that the 1898-1900 books may be issued to them as soon as the editions are finisht. The Society's experience has shown that Editors must be taken when they are in the humour for work. All real Students and furtherers of the Society's purpose will be ready to push-on the issue of Texts. Those Members who care only a guinea a year (or can afford only that sum) for the history of our language and our nation's thought, will not be hurt by those who care more, getting their books in advance ; on the contrary, they will be benefited, as each successive year's work will then be ready for issue on New Year's Day. Members are askt to realise the fact that the Society has now 50 years' work on its Lists,—at its present rate of production,—and that there is from 100 to 200 more years' work to come after that. The year 2000 will not see finisht all the Texts that the Society ought to print.

Mr. G. N. Currie is preparing an edition of the 15th and 16th century Prose Versions of Guillaume de Deguilleville's *Pilgrimage of the Life of Man,* with the French prose version by Jean Gallopes, from Lord Aldenham's MS., Lord Aldenham having generously promist to pay the extra cost of printing the French text, and engraving one or two of the illuminations in his MS.

Guillaume de Deguilleville, monk of the Cistercian abbey of Chaalis, in the diocese of Senlis, wrote his first verse *Pelerinaige de l'Homme* in 1330-1 when he was 36.[1] Twenty-five (or six) years after, in 1355, he revised his poem, and issued a second version of it, and this is the only one that has been printed. Of the prose representative of the first version, 1330-1, a prose Englishing, about 1430 A.D., was edited by Mr. Aldis Wright for the Roxburghe Club in 1869, from MS. Ff. 5. 30 in the Cambridge University Library. Other copies of this prose English are in the Hunterian Museum, Glasgow, Q. 2. 25 ; Univ. Coll. and Corpus Christi, Oxford[2]; and the Laud Collection in the Bodleian, no. 740. A copy in the Northern dialect is MS. G. 21, in St. John's Coll., Cambridge, and this is the MS. which will be edited by Mr. Sidney J. Herrtage for the E. E. Text Society. The Laud MS. 740 was somewhat condenst and modernised, in the 17th century, into MS. Ff. 6. 30, in the Cambridge University Library:[3] "The Pilgrime or the Pilgrimage of Man in this World," copied by Will. Baspoole, whose copy "was verbatim written by Walter Parker, 1645, and from thence transcribed by G. G. 1649 ; and from thence by W. A. 1655." This last copy may have been read by, or its story reported to, Bunyan, and may have been the groundwork of his *Pilgrim's Progress.* It will be edited by Mr. Currie for the E. E. T. Soc., its text running under the earlier English, as in Mr. Herrtage's edition of the *Gesta Romanorum* for the Society. In February 1464,[4] Jean Gallopes—a clerk of Angers, afterwards chaplain to John, Duke of Bedford, Regent of France—turned Deguilleville's first verse *Pelerinaige* into a prose *Pelerinage de la vie humaine.*[5] By the kindness of Lord Aldenham, as above mentiond, Gallopes's French text will be printed opposite the early prose northern Englishing in the Society's edition.

---

[1] He was born about 1295. See Abbé Goujet's *Bibliothèque française,* Vol. IX, p. 73-4,—P. M.
[2] The 3 MSS. have not yet been collated, but are believed to be all of the same version.
[3] Another MS. is in the Pepys Library.
[4] According to Mr. Hy. Hucks Gibbs's MS.
[5] These were printed in France, late in the 15th or early in the 16th century.

The Second Version of Deguilleville's *Pelerinaige de l'Homme*, A.D. 1355 or -6, was englisht in verse by Lydgate in 1426. Of Lydgate's poem, the larger part is in the Cotton MS. Vitellius C. xiii (leaves 2-308). This MS. leaves out Chaucer's englishing of Deguilleville's *A B C* or *Prayer to the Virgin*, of which the successive stanzas start with A, B, C, and run all thro' the alphabet; and it has 2 gaps, of which most of the second can be fild up from the end of the other imperfect MS. Cotton, Tiberius A vii. The rest of the stopgaps must be got from the original French in Harleian 4399,[1] and Additional 22,937[2] and 25,594[3] in the British Museum. Lydgate's version will be edited in due course for the Society.

Besides his first *Pelerinaige de l'homme* in its two versions, Deguilleville wrote a second, "de l'ame separee du corps," and a third, "de nostre seigneur Iesus." Of the second, a prose Englishing of 1413, *The Pilgrimage of the Sowle* (perhaps in part by Lydgate), exists in the Egerton MS. 615,[4] at Hatfield, Cambridge (Univ. Kk. 1. 7, Caius), Oxford (Univ. Coll. and Corpus), and in Caxton's edition of 1483. This version has 'somewhat of addicions' as Caxton says, and some shortenings too, as the maker of both, the first translator, tells us in the MSS. Caxton leaves out the earlier englisher's interesting Epilog in the Egerton MS. This prose englishing of the *Sowle* will be edited for the Society after that of the *Man* is finisht, and will have Gallopes's French opposite it, from Lord Aldenham's MS., as his gift to the Society. Of the Pilgrimage of Jesus, no englishing is known.

As to the MS. Anglo-Saxon Psalters, Dr. Hy. Sweet has edited the oldest MS., the Vespasian, in his *Oldest English Texts* for the Society, and Mr. Harsley has edited the latest, c. 1150, Eadwine's Canterbury Psalter. The other MSS., except the Paris one, being interlinear versions,—some of the Roman-Latin redaction, and some of the Gallican,—Prof. Logeman has prepared for press, a Parallel-Text edition of the first twelve Psalms, to start the complete work. He will do his best to get the Paris Psalter—tho' it is not an interlinear one—into this collective edition; but the additional matter, especially in the Verse-Psalms, is very difficult to manage. If the Paris text cannot be parallelised, it will form a separate volume. The Early English Psalters are all independent versions, and will follow separately in due course.

Through the good offices of the Examiners, some of the books for the Early-English Examinations of the University of London will be chosen from the Society's publications, the Committee having undertaken to supply such books to students at a large reduction in price. The profits from these sales, after the payment of costs arising out of the issuing of such Texts to Students, will be applied to the Society's Reprints. Five of its 1866 Texts, and one of its 1867 (now at press), still need reproducing. Donations for this purpose will be welcome. They should be paid to the Hon. Sec., Mr. W. A. Dalziel, 67 Victoria Rd., Finsbury Park, London, N.

Members are reminded that *fresh Subscribers are always wanted*, and that the Committee can at any time, on short notice, send to press an additional Thousand Pounds' worth of work.

The Subscribers to the Original Series must be prepared for the issue of the whole of the Early English *Lives of Saints*, sooner or later. The Society cannot leave out any of them, even though some are dull. The Sinners would doubtless be much more interesting. But in many Saints' Lives will be found valuable incidental details of our forefathers' social state, and all are worthful for the history of our language. The Lives may be lookt on as the religious romances or story-books of their period.

The Standard Collection of Saints' Lives in the Corpus and Ashmole MSS., the Harleian MS. 2277, &c. will repeat the Laud set, our No. 87, with additions, and in right order. (The foundation MS. (Laud 108) had to be printed first, to prevent quite unwieldy collations.) The Supplementary Lives from the Vernon and other MSS. will form one or two separate volumes.

Besides the Saints' Lives, Trevisa's englishing of *Bartholomæus de Proprietatibus Rerum*, the mediæval Cyclopædia of Science, &c., will be the Society's next big undertaking. Dr. R. von Fleischhacker will edit it. Prof. Napier of Oxford, wishing to have the whole of our MS. Anglo-Saxon in type, and accessible to students, will edit for the Society all the unprinted and other Anglo-Saxon Homilies which are not included in Thorpe's edition of Ælfric's prose,[5] Dr. Morris's of the Blickling Homilies, and Prof. Skeat's of Ælfric's Metrical Homilies. Prof. Kölbing has also undertaken for the Society's Extra Series a Parallel-Text of all the six MSS. of the *Ancren Riwle*, one of the most important foundation-documents of

---

[1] 15th cent., containing only the *Vie humaine.*
[2] 15th cent., containing all the 3 Pilgrimages, the 3rd being Jesus Christ's.
[3] 14th cent., containing the *Vie humaine* and the 2nd Pilgrimage, *de l'Ame*: both incomplete.
[4] Ab. 1430, 106 leaves (leaf 1 of text wanting), with illuminations of nice little devils—red, green, tawny &c.—and damnd souls, fires, angels &c.
[5] Of these, Mr. Harsley is preparing a new edition, with collations of all the MSS. Many copies of Thorpe's book, not issued by the Ælfric Society, are still in stock.
Of the Vercell Homilies, the Society has bought the copy made by Prof. G. Lattanzi.

Early English. Mr. Harvey, too, means to prepare an edition of the three MSS. of the *Earliest English Metrical Psalter*, one of which was edited by the late Mr. Stevenson for the Surtees Society.

In case more Texts are ready at any time than can be paid for by the current year's income, they will be dated the next year, and issued in advance to such Members as will pay advance subscriptions. The 1886-7 delay in getting out Texts must not occur again, if it can possibly be avoided. The Director has in hand for future volunteer Editors, copies of 2 or 3 MSS.

Members of the Society will learn with pleasure that its example has been followed, not only by the Old French Text Society which has done such admirable work under its founders Profs. Paul Meyer and Gaston Paris, but also by the Early Russian Text Society, which was set on foot in 1877, and has since issued many excellent editions of old MS. Chronicles &c.

Members will also note with pleasure the annexation of large tracts of our Early English territory by the important German contingent under General Zupitza, Colonel Kölbing, volunteers Hausknecht, Einenkel, Haenisch, Kaluza, Hupe, Adam, Holthausen, Schick, Herzfeld, Brandeis, &c. Scandinavia has also sent us Prof. Erdmann ; Holland, Prof. H. Logeman, who is now working in Belgium ; France, Prof. Paul Meyer—with Gaston Paris as adviser ; — Italy, Prof. Lattanzi ; Hungary, Dr. von Fleischhacker ; while America is represented by Prof. Child, Dr. Mary Noyes Colvin, Profs. Mead, Perrin, McClintock, Triggs, &c. The sympathy, the ready help, which the Society's work has call forth from the Continent and the United States, have been among the pleasantest experiences of the Society's life, a real aid and cheer amid all troubles and discouragements. All our Members are grateful for it, and recognise that the bond their work has woven between them and the lovers of language and antiquity across the seas is one of the most welcome results of the Society's efforts.

ORIGINAL SERIES.

Half the Publications for 1866 (13, 14, 15, 18, 22) are out of print, but will be gradually reprinted. Subscribers who desire the issue for 1866 should send their guineas at once to the Hon. Secretary, in order that other Texts for 1866 may be sent to press.

The Publications for 1864-1897 (*one guinea each year, save those for 1866 now half out of print, two guineas*) are :—

1. Early English Alliterative Poems, ab. 1360 A.D., ed. Rev. Dr. R. Morris. 16s.	1864
2. Arthur, ab. 1440, ed. F. J. Furnivall, M.A. 4s.	,,
3. Lauder on the Dewtie of Kyngis, &c., 1556, ed. F. Hall, D.C.L. 4s.	,,
4. Sir Gawayne and the Green Knight, ab. 1360, ed. Rev. Dr. R. Morris. 10s.	,,
5. Hume's Orthographie and Congruitie of the Britan Tongue, ab 1617, ed. H. B. Wheatley. 4s.	1865
6. Lancelot of the Laik, ab. 1500, ed. Rev. W. W. Skeat. 8s	,,
7. Genesis & Exodus, ab. 1250, ed. Rev. Dr. R. Morris. 8s.	,,
8. Morte Arthure, ab. 1440, ed. E. Brock. 7s.	,,
9. Thynne on Speght's ed. of Chaucer, A.D. 1599, ed. Dr. G. Kingsley and Dr. F. J. Furnivall. 10s.	,,
10. Merlin, ab. 1440, Part I., ed. H. B. Wheatley. 2s. 6d.	,,
11. Lyndesay's Monarche, &c., 1552, Part I., ed. J. Small, M.A. 3s.	,,
12. Wright's Chaste Wife, ab. 1462, ed. F. J. Furnivall, M.A. 1s.	,,
13. Seinte Marherete, 1200-1330, ed. Rev. O. Cockayne : to be re-edited by Prof. Herford, M.A., Ph.D.	1866
14. Kyng Horn, Floris and Blancheflour, &c., ed. Rev. J. R. Lumby, B.D.	,,
15. Political, Religious, and Love Poems, ed. F. J. Furnivall.	,,
16. The Book of Quinte Essence, ab. 1460-70, ed. F. J. Furnivall. 1s. [*In print.*]	,,
17. Parallel Extracts from 45 MSS. of Piers the Plowman, ed. Rev. W. W. Skeat. 1s. [*In print.*]	,,
18. Hali Meidenhad, ab. 1200, ed. Rev. O. Cockayne.	,,
19. Lyndesay's Monarche, &c., Part II., ed. J. Small, M.A. 3s. 6d. [*In print.*]	,,
20. Hampole's English Prose Treatises, ed. Rev. G. G. Perry. 1s. [*In print.*]	,,
21. Merlin, Part II., ed. H. B. Wheatley. 4s. [*In print.*]	,,
22. Partenay or Lusignen, ed. Rev. W. W. Skeat.	,,
23. Dan Michel's Ayenbite of Inwyt, 1340, ed. Rev. Dr. R. Morris. 10s. 6d. [*In print.*]	,,
24. Hymns to the Virgin and Christ ; the Parliament of Devils, &c., ab. 1430, ed. F. J. Furnivall. [*At Press.* 1867
25. The Stacions of Rome, the Pilgrims' Sea-voyage, with Clene Maydenhod, ed. F. J. Furnivall. 1s.	,,
26. Religious Pieces in Prose and Verse, from R. Thornton's MS. (ab. 1440', ed. Rev. G. G. Perry. 2s.	,,
27. Levins's Manipulus Vocabulorum, a ryming Dictionary, 1570, ed. H. B. Wheatley. 12s.	,,
28. William's Vision of Piers the Plowman, 1362 A.D. ; Text A, Part I., ed. Rev. W. W. Skeat. 6s.	,,
29. Old English Homilies (ab. 1220-30 A.D.). Part I. Edited by Rev. Dr. R. Morris. 7s.	,,
30. Pierce the Ploughmans Crede, ed. Rev. W. W. Skeat. 2s.	,,

EXTRA SERIES.

The Publications for 1867-1895 (one guinea each year) are :—

XX. Lonelich's Holy Grail, ed. F. J. Furnivall, M.A., Ph.D. Part IV. 15s.   1878
XXI. The Alliterative Romance of Alexander and Dindimus, ed. Rev. W. W. Skeat. 6s.   ,,
XXII. Starkey's "England in Henry VIII's time." Pt. I. Starkey's Life and Letters, ed. S. J. Herrtage. 8s. ,,
XXIII. Gesta Romanorum (englisht ab. 1440), ed. S. J. Herrtage, B.A. 15s.   1879
XXIV. The Charlemagne Romances:—1. Sir Ferumbras, from Ashm. MS. 33, ed. S. J. Herrtage. 15s.   ,,
XXV. Charlemagne Romances:—2. The Sege off Melayne, Sir Otuell, &c., ed. S. J. Herrtage. 12s.   1880
XXVI. Charlemagne Romances:—3. Lyf of Charles the Grete, Pt. I., ed. S. J. Herrtage. 16s.   ,,
XXVII. Charlemagne Romances:—4. Lyf of Charles the Grete, Pt. II., ed. S. J. Herrtage. 15s.   1881
XXVIII. Charlemagne Romances:—5. The Sowdone of Babylone, ed. Dr. Hausknecht. 15s.   ,,
XXIX. Charlemagne Romances:—6. Rauf Colyear, Roland, Otuel, &c., ed. S. J. Herrtage, B.A. 15s.   1882
XL. Charlemagne Romances:—7. Huon of Burdeux, by Lord Berners, ed. S. L. Lee, B.A. Part I. 15s.   ,,
XLI. Charlemagne Romances:—8. Huon of Burdeux, by Lord Berners, ed. S. L. Lee, B.A. Pt. II. 15s. 1883
XLII. Guy of Warwick: 2 texts (Auchinleck MS. and Caius MS.), ed. Prof. Zupitza. Part I. 15s.   ,,
XLIII. Charlemagne Romances:—9. Huon of Burdeux, by Lord Berners, ed. S. L. Lee, B.A. Pt. III. 15s. 1884
XLIV. Charlemagne Romances:—10. The Four Sons of Aymon, ed. Miss Octavia Richardson. Pt. I. 15s. ,,
XLV. Charlemagne Romances:—11. The Four Sons of Aymon, ed. Miss O. Richardson. Pt. II. 20s. 1885
XLVI. Sir Bevis of Hamton, from the Auchinleck and other MSS., ed. Prof. E. Kölbing, Ph.D. Part I. 10s. ,,
XLVII. The Wars of Alexander, ed. Rev. Prof. Skeat, Litt.D., LL.D. 20s.   1886
XLVIII. Sir Bevis of Hamton, ed. Prof. E. Kölbing, Ph.D. Part II. 10s.   ,,
XLIX. Guy of Warwick, 2 texts (Auchinleck and Caius MSS.), Pt. II., ed. Prof. J. Zupitza, Ph.D. 15s. 1887 '
L. Charlemagne Romances:—12. Huon of Burdeux, by Lord Berners, ed. S. L. Lee, B.A. Part IV. 5s. ,,
LI. Torrent of Portyngale, from the unique MS. in the Chetham Library, ed. E. Adam, Ph.D. 10s. ,,
LII. Bullein's Dialogue against the Feuer Pestilence, 1578 (ed. 1, 1564). Ed. M. & A. H. Bullen. 10s. 1888
LIII. Vicary's Anatomie of the Body of Man, 1548, ed. 1577, ed. F. J. & Percy Furnivall. Part I. 15s. ,,
LIV. Caxton's Englishing of Alain Chartier's Curial, ed. Dr. F. J. Furnivall & Prof. P. Meyer. 5s. ,,
LV. Barbour's Bruce, ed. Rev. Prof. Skeat, Litt.D., LL.D. Part IV. 5s.   1889
LVI. Early English Pronunciation, by A. J. Ellis, Esq., F.R.S. Pt. V., the present English Dialects. 25s. ,,
LVII. Caxton's Eneydos, A.D. 1490, coll. with its French, ed. M. T. Culley, M.A. & Dr. F. J. Furnivall. 13s. 1890
LVIII. Caxton's Blanchardyn & Eglantine, c. 1489, extracts from ed. 1595, & French, ed. Dr. L. Kellner. 17s. ,,
LIX. Guy of Warwick, 2 texts (Auchinleck and Caius MSS.), Part III., ed. Prof. J. Zupitza, Ph.D. 15s. 1891
LX. Lydgate's Temple of Glass, re-edited from the MSS. by Dr. J. Schick. 15s.   ,,
LXI. Hoccleve's Minor Poems, I., from the Phillipps and Durham MSS., ed. F. J. Furnivall, Ph.D. 15s. 1892
LXII. The Chester Plays, re-edited from the MSS. by the late Dr. Hermann Deimling. Part I. 15s. ,,
LXIII. Thomas a Kempis's De Imitatione Christi, englisht ab. 1440, & 1502, ed. Prof. J. K. Ingram. 15s. 1893
LXIV. Caxton's Godfrey of Boloyne, or Last Siege of Jerusalem, 1481, ed. Dr. Mary N. Colvin. 15s. ,,
LXV. Sir Bevis of Hamton, ed. Prof. E. Kölbing, Ph.D. Part III. 15s.   1894
LXVI. Lydgate's and Burgh's Secrees of Philisoffres. ab. 1445—50, ed. R. Steele, B.A. 15s.   ,,
LXVII. The Three Kings' Sons, a Romance, ab. 1500, Part I., the Text, ed. Dr. Furnivall. 10s.   1895
LXVIII. Melusine, the prose Romance, ab. 1500, Part I, the Text, ed. A. K. Donald. 20s.   ,,
LXIX. Lydgate's Assembly of the Gods, ed. Prof. Oscar L. Triggs, M.A., Ph.D. 15s.   1896
LXX. The Digby Plays, edited by Dr. F. J. Furnivall. 15s.   ,,
LXXI. The Towneley Plays, ed. Geo. England and A. W. Pollard, M.A. 15s.   1897
LXXII. Hoccleve's Regement of Princes, 1411-12, edited by Dr. F. J. Furnivall. 15s.   ,,
LXXIII. ? Hoccleve's Minor Poems, II., from the Ashburnham MS., ed. I. Gollancz, M.A. [*At Press.* ,,
? Melusine, the Prose Romance, ab. 1500, Part II., Introduction by A. K. Donald. 10s.   1898
? Promptorium Parvulorum, c. 1440, from the Winchester MS., ed. Rev. A. L. Mayhew, M.A. Part I. 20s. ,,

---

EARLY ENGLISH TEXT SOCIETY TEXTS PREPARING.

Besides the Texts named as at press on p. 12 of the Cover of the Early English Text Society's last books, the following Texts are also slowly preparing for the Society :—

ORIGINAL SERIES.

Thomas Robinson's Life and Death of Mary Magdalene, from the 2 MSS., ab. 1620 A.D. (*Text in type.*)
The Earliest English Prose Psalter, ed. Dr. K. D. Buelbring. Part II.
The Earliest English Verse Psalter, 3 texts, ed. Rev. R. Harvey, M.A.
Anglo-Saxon Poems, from the Vercelli MS., re-edited by I. Gollancz, M.A.
Anglo-Saxon Glosses to Latin Prayers and Hymns, edited by Dr. F. Holthausen.
Aelfric's Metrical Lives of Saints, MS. Cott. Jul. E 7, Part IV, ed. Prof. Skeat, Litt.D., LL.D.
All the Anglo-Saxon Homilies and Lives of Saints not accessible in English editions, including those of the Vercelli MS. &c., edited by Prof. Napier, M.A., Ph.D.
The Anglo-Saxon Psalms; all the MSS. in Parallel Texts, ed. Dr. H. Logeman and F. Harsley, B.A.
Beowulf, a critical Text, &c., edited by a Pupil of the late Prof. Zupitza, Ph.D.
Byrhtferth's Handboc, edited by Prof. G. Hempl.
The Secret of Secrets, 3 prose versions from MSS, 2 at Lambeth, and one by Jas. Younge, 1420, ed. R. Steele, B.A.
The Rule of St. Benet: 5 Texts, Anglo-Saxon, Early English, Caxton, &c. (*Editor wanted.*)

The Seven Sages, in the Northern Dialect, from a Cotton MS., edited by Dr. Squires.
The Master of the Game, a Book of Huntynge for Hen. V. when Prince of Wales. (*Editor wanted.*)
Ailred's Rule of Nuns, &c., edited from the Vernon MS., by the Rev. Canon H. R. Bramley, M.A.
Lonelich's Merlin (verse), from the unique MS., ed. by Prof. E. Kölbing, Ph.D.
Merlin (prose), Part IV., containing Preface, Index, and Glossary. Edited by Prof. W. E. Mead, Ph.D.
Early English Verse Lives of Saints, Standard Collection, from the Harl. MS.
Early English Confessionals, edited by Dr. R. von Fleischhacker.
A Lapidary, from Lord Tollemache's MS., &c., edited by Dr. R. von Fleischhacker.
Early English Deeds and Documents, from unique MSS., ed. Dr. Lorenz Morsbach.
Gilbert Banastre's Poems, and other Boccaccio englishings, ed. by a pupil of the late Prof. J. Zupitza, Ph.D.
Lanfranc's Cirurgie, ab. 1400 A.D., ed. Dr. R. von Fleischhacker, Part II.
William of Nassington's Mirror of Life, from Jn. of Waldby, edited by J. T. Herbert, M.A.
A Chronicle of England to 1327 A.D., Northern verse (42,000 lines), ab. 1400 A.D., ed. M. L. Perrin, B.A.
More Early English Wills from the Probate Registry at Somerset House. (*Editor Wanted.*)
Early Lincoln Wills and Documents from the Bishops' Registers, &c., edited by Dr. F. J. Furnivall.
Early Canterbury Wills, edited by William Cowper, B.A., and J. Meadows Cowper.
Early Norwich Wills, edited by Walter Rye, and F. J. Furnivall.
The Cartularies of Oseney Abbey and Godstow Nunnery, englisht ab. 1450, ed. Rev. A. Clark, M.A.
The Macro Moralities, edited from Mr. Gurney's unique MS., by Alfred W. Pollard, M.A.
A Troy-Book, edited from the unique Laud MS. 595, by Dr. E. Wülfing.
Alliterative Prophecies, edited from the MSS. by Prof. Brandl, Ph. D.
Miscellaneous Alliterative Poems, edited from the MSS. by Dr. L. Morsbach.
Bird and Beast Poems, a collection from MSS., edited by Dr. K. D. Buelbring.
Scire Mori, &c., from the Lichfield MS. 16, ed. Mrs. L. Grindon, LL.A., and Miss Florence Gilbert.
Nicholas Trivet's French Chronicle, from Sir A. Acland-Hood's unique MS., ed. by Miss Mary Bateson.
Stories for Sermons, edited from the Addit. MS. 25,719 by Dr. Wieck of Coblentz.
Early English Homilies in Harl. 2276 &c., c. 1400, ed. J. Friedländer.
Extracts from the Registers of Boughton, ed. Hy. Littlehales, Esq.
The Diary of Prior Moore of Worcester, A.D. 1518-35, from the unique MS., ed. Henry Littlehales, Esq.
The Pore Caitif, edited from its MSS., by Mr. Peake.

EXTRA SERIES.

De Guilleville's Pilgrimage of the Sowle, edited by G. N. Currie, M.A.
Vicary's Anatomie, 1548, from the unique MS. copy by George Jeans, edited by F. J. & Percy Furnivall.
Vicary's Anatomie, 1548, ed. 1577, edited by F. J. & Percy Furnivall. Part II. [*At Press.*
Bp. Fisher's English Works, Pt. II., with his Life and Letters, ed. Rev. Ronald Bayne, B.A. [*At Press.*
William Staunton's St. Patrick's Purgatory, &c., ed. J. T. Herbert, M.A.
A Parallel-text of the 6 MSS. of the Ancren Riwle, ed. Prof. Dr. E. Kölbing.
Trevisa's Bartholomæus de Proprietatibus Rerum, re-edited by Dr. R. von Fleischhacker.
Bullein's Dialogue against the Feuer Pestilence, 1564, 1573, 1578. Ed. A. H. and M. Bullen. Pt. II.
The Romance of Boctus and Sidrac, edited from the MSS. by Dr. K. D. Buelbring.
The Romance of Clariodus, re-edited by Dr. K. D. Buelbring.
Sir Amadas, re-edited from the MSS. by Dr. K. D. Buelbring.
Sir Degrevant, edited from the MSS. by Dr. K. Luick.
Robert of Brunne's Chronicle of England, from the Inner Temple MS., ed. by Prof. W. E. Mead, Ph.D.
Maundeville's Voiage and Travaile, re-edited from the Cotton MS. Titus C. 16, &c., by Miss M. Bateson.
Avowynge of Arthur, re-edited from the unique Ireland MS. by Dr. K. D. Buelbring.
Guy of Warwick, Copland's version, edited by a pupil of the late Prof. Zupitza, Ph.D.
The Sege of Jerusalem, Text A, edited from the MSS. by Prof. Dr. E. Kölbing.
Liber Fundacionis Ecclesie Sancti Bartholomei Londoniarum : englisht ab. 1425, ed. Norman Moore, M.D.
Awdelay's Poems, re-edited from the unique MS. Douce 302, by Dr. E. Wülfing.
William of Shoreham's Works, re-edited by Professor Konrath, Ph.D.
The Wyse Chylde and other early Treatises on Education, Northwich School, Harl. 2099 &c., ed. G. Collar, B.A.
Caxton's Dictes and Sayengis of Philosophirs, 1477, with Lord Tollemache's MS. version, ed. S. I. Butler, Esq.
Caxton's Book of the Ordre of Chyualry, collated with Loutfut's Scotch copy, ed. F. S. Ellis, Esq.
Lydgate's Court of Sapience, edited by Dr. Borsdorf.
Lydgate's Lyfe of oure Lady, ed. by Prof. Georg Fiedler, Ph.D.
Lydgate's Reason and Sensuality, englisht from the French, edited by Dr. Sieper.
Lydgate's Dance of Death, edited by Miss Florence Warren.
Lydgate's Life of St. Edmund, edited from the MSS. by Dr. Axel Erdmann.
Richard Cœur de Lion, re-edited from Harl. MS. 4690, by Prof. Hausknecht, Ph.D.
The Romance of Athelstan, re-edited by a pupil of the late Prof. J. Zupitza, Ph.D.
The Romance of Sir Degare, re-edited by Dr. Breul.
Mulcaster's Positions 1581, and Elementarie 1582, ed. Dr. Th. Klaehr, Dresden.
Caxton's Recuyell of the Histories of Troye, edited by H. Halliday Sparling.
Walton's verse Boethius de Consolatione, edited by Mark H. Liddell, U. S. A.
The Gospel of Nichodemus, edited by Ernest Riedel.

The Society is anxious to hear of more early Dialect MSS. John Lacy's copy, in the Newcastle-on-Tyne dialect, 1434, of some theological tracts in MS. 94 of St. John's College, Oxford, is to be edited by Prof. McClintock. More Hampoles in the Yorkshire dialect will follow. The Lincoln and Norfolk Wills, already copied by or for Dr. Furnivall, unluckily show but little traces of dialect.

More members (to bring money) and Editors (to bring brains) are wanted by the Society.

Any member who may desire to bind with his copy of the Chevelere Assigne, the photographs of the Casket referred to in the Preface, will receive them ready mounted for binding, on sending to Mr Blanchard, No. 12, Camden Cottages, N.W., 1s. 9d. in postage stamps for demys-paper, or 2s. for large-paper copies.

The Romance

of the

Cheuelere Assigne.

Early English Text Society.

Extra Series. No. VI.

1868.

BERLIN: ASHER & CO., 13, UNTER DEN LINDEN.

NEW YORK: C. SCRIBNER & CO.: LEYPOLDT & HOLT.

PHILADELPHIA: J. B. LIPPINCOTT & CO.

The Romance

of the

Chevelere Assigne.

———•——

RE-EDITED FROM

THE UNIQUE MANUSCRIPT IN THE BRITISH MUSEUM,

WITH A PREFACE, NOTES, AND GLOSSARIAL INDEX,

BY

HENRY H. GIBBS, ESQ., M.A.,

OF EXETER COLLEGE, OXFORD.

———•——

LONDON:

PUBLISHED FOR THE EARLY ENGLISH TEXT SOCIETY

BY KEGAN PAUL, TRENCH, TRÜBNER & Co.,

PATERNOSTER HOUSE, CHARING-CROSS ROAD, W.C.

MDCCCLXVIII.

[*Reprinted 1898.*]

Extra Series, VI.

R. CLAY & SONS, LIMITED, LONDON & BUNGAY.

PREFACE.

This short alliterative poem has already been edited by Mr Utterson, and presented by him in 1820 to the members of the Roxburghe Club; but as the few copies then printed are very rare, and as the work is a curious specimen of unrimed alliterative poetry of a comparatively late date, it has been thought worth while that it should be edited again for the Extra Series of the Early English Text Society.

A mere reprint of the former edition would not have been desirable, both because there are several mistranscriptions, and because the glossary appended to that edition is excessively meagre, and in some cases erroneous: but so much advance has been made since the date of that publication in the knowledge of our ancient tongue, that however much this edition may leave to be desired, there will be no great difficulty in correcting the errors of the former one.

Wherever the new transcript differed from the Roxburghe edition, I have with especial care compared it with the manuscript, so as to satisfy myself of the correctness of the new reading.

The poem consists of 370 lines; and is contained, with other pieces, in Caligula A. 2 of the Cotton MSS. in the British Museum. It professes to be taken from some other book (in the 7th line and elsewhere the author uses the expression, 'as þe book tellethe'), and appears to be an epitome of the first 1083 lines of the French poem, or rather 'lay'.(in the sense in which Scott uses the word), which forms part of the volume marked 15 E. vj in the Royal Collection in the same library.

This French Manuscript contains many beautiful illuminations of excellent workmanship, two of which adorn the head of the first page (fo. 320) of the 'Chevalier au Signe.' The left-hand picture represents Queen Bietrix (as she is there called) sitting up in bed and looking very unhappy, while 'Matebrune' is carrying away a cot (nearly as big as the Queen's bed) with the seven children in it, clad four in green and three in purple, placed alternately. The right-hand picture represents the Knight 'Helyas,' armed, and in his ship alone; the

Swan, 'ducally gorged, Or,' as a herald would say, sailing proudly before him. This picture is very like one of the compartments of the Ivory Casket, to which I shall presently refer.

Meanwhile, as this French chanson—so its author frequently calls it [1]—appears to be the original from whence our English author drew his poem, I will give an outline of the longer history told in its 6000 lines, comparing it from time to time with the very entertaining English Prose Romance, printed by Copland early in the 16th century, and edited in 1858 by Mr Thoms.

THE STORY OF THE KNIGHT OF THE SWAN.

Briefly told it is as follows :

Beatrix, Queen of King Oryens of Lilefort, after some years of childlessness, conceived seven children at one burden (as a punishment for disbelieving the possibility of twins being begotten by one man) ; and when she is brought to bed, in her husband's absence, his mother substitutes seven puppies for the seven children, whom she consigns to Marques, or Marcon, a serf of hers, with orders for their murder : when the King returns she shows him the whelps as the Queen's offspring, and demands her death ; but the King only allows her to be imprisoned.

The children (who were miraculously born with silver chains about their necks) are of course not slain, but fed by a hind in the forest, and tended by a hermit in his cell.

They are unfortunately seen by the Forester Mauquarre, or Malquarrez, who tells the Queen ; and by her desire he goes back to kill them and take away their chains. One, however, who is the hero of the tale, has gone out with the hermit to get food for the others ; so that the forester finds only six of the children, and deprives them of their chains, upon which they are transformed into swans.

---

[1] The poem begins ' *Escoutez seigneurs pour Dieu lespitable*
     Que Ihus vous garisse de lamain au Dyable ; '
and every now and then the minstrel addresses his hearers to call their attention to his song. Thus when Elyas first comes to Nimaye, the next sentence begins ' *Seigneurs oez chancon qui moult fait aloer.*' After the battle with the friends of the prevost, comes, ' *Seigneurs or escoutez chancon de grant baronaige ;* ' and again, ' *Seigneurs or escoutez bonne chancon ;* ' and ' *Seigneurs oez chancon de bonne enluminee ;* ' and ' *Seigneurs oyez chancon qui est vray.*'

The old Queen questions Marcon, and revenges herself on him by putting out his eyes.

When the Queen has been 11 years in prison, Matebrune prevails on the King to condemn her to be burnt; and the day is fixed accordingly, and she is led to the stake.

Meanwhile an angel appears to the hermit and orders that the child should go to the city, be christened Helyas, and fight for his mother. He does so, meets the procession, accosts the King, obtains his consent to the battle, borrows from him horse and armour, slays Mauquarre, who is the champion on behalf of the accuser, and frees his mother.

Matebrune flees to a castle; Helyas prays to God, who restores Marques's sight. He tells his story to his newly-found father and mother, and all the court go to the water where the swans are swimming, and, their chains being restored to them, they resume their human form; all but one, who remains a swan.

Up to this time, as will be seen, the English poem faithfully accompanies the French one, excepting that as the poet means to make an end here, he summarily burns Matabryne, and says that the 6th brother continued *always* a swan for lack of his chain.

Moreover he makes no mention of the miracle of healing done on Marcus.

The French story proceeds with the abdication of King Oriant (on the plea that he has now lived a long time—*plus que c. ans*—) in favour of Helyas; with the siege of Matebrune's castle, the death of her champion Hendrys by the hand of Helyas; her capture, confession, and burning; whereafter

'*Lame emporterent dyables; ce fut la destinee.*'

The angel then appears to King Helyas and bids him leave his father and mother, and seek adventures under the guidance of his brother the swan, who waits for him with '*ung batel.*'

He abdicates, and leaves the kingdom to Orions, and divers governments to his other brothers.

From this differs the English Prose Romance of the Knight of the Swan, which makes no mention of King Oryens' great age, but makes

King Helyas surrender the kingdom again into his hands. Neither does he mention Helyas's departure at the bidding of the angel; but makes the swan-brother summon him by 'mervaylous cries,' to come into the boat which he has brought, and which he guides, without further adventure, to the city of Nimaye.

But in the French story he arrives soon at a city of Saracens, who assault him and his swan;—but he is rescued by 30 galleys under the guidance of Saint George (*qui fut bon chevalier*); and the four winds also helped, raising a storm and drowning the Saracens.

It then tells how Elyas went on alone in his boat, with the swan, till they came to a castle, called Sauvage, whose master was Agolant, brother of Matebrune; how their provisions being exhausted, they sought help at the castle; how Agolant received him well, but, after hearing his story, seizes, imprisons, and promises to burn him eight days thereafter.

But a page escapes and goes to Lilefort to King Orions, who goes with a great force to succour his brother. The men arrive when Helyas is already bound at the stake, and Agolant and all his men have to go out to repel them;—a friendly hand releases Helyas, who joins his brother's men, and slays Agolant.

Oryons goes back to Lilefort, and Helyas, summoning his brother the swan, pursues his way to Nimaye.

There, in a tournament, he slays an Earl [of Francbourck, says Copland], who, in a false plea before the Emperor Otho, is trying to deprive [Clarysse] Duchess Dabullon [of Bouillon] of her lands; and wins for himself the lands of Ardennes [of Dardaigne, in Copland] belonging to the Earl; and also gets to wife Beatrice, the fair daughter and heiress of the Duchess, by whom he has a daughter Idein or Ydain, who in time becomes the mother of Godfrey of Bouillon.

He leaves Nimaye and goes to his duchy of Bouillon, conquering in the way *Asselm le prevost* and many partisans of the deceased Earl, who had laid an ambush for him.

Many perilous adventures then befell him in Bouillon, which are recounted at considerable length; and afterwards the story tells how that, his wife having disobeyed his commandment which he laid upon her, not to inquire concerning his kith and kin, he departs from her, and rides away to Nimaye, to take leave of the Emperor, and bespeak his protection for his wife, daughter, and lands.

Thence, amidst great lamentation of the Emperor and all his barons, he departs in his boat with his brother the swan, and no more is known of him.

Oncq ne sceurent quelle part y fu tournes.

Then it passes on to tell of Godfrey Earl of Bouillon, his birth and deeds. How with the leave of the Emperor, Eustace Earl of ' *Boulogne sur mer salee* ' went a courting to Ydain ' *a la fresce coulour* ' (daughter of Helyas), then aged 13 years; how he married her; and how in the three years following she had three fair sons, Godfrey, Baldwin, and Eustace; and how that the eldest after many noble deeds went to Palestine, and took the Holy City. The poem ends with the assault and capture of Jerusalem and the crowning of Godfrey as its King.

The English Prose Romance takes up the story of Helyas where the French Poem leaves him, and tells how he arrived at Lilefort and is welcomed by his father and mother after his viij years' absence.

The Queen, it tells us, had a dream, in which she dreams that if they get the two cups which had been made of the 6th son's chain, and lay them on two altars, and set the swan on a bed betwixt the altars, and cause two masses to be said by devout priests who shall consecrate in the two chalices, the swan shall return to his own form: and ' Ryght so,' says Copland, ' as the priests consacred the body of our Lorde at the masse, the swanne retourned into his propre fourme and was a man,' and he was baptized, and named Emery.

' The whiche sith was a noble knight.'

' And thus,' he says, ' the noble king Oriant and the good queene Beatrice finabli recovered all their children by the grace of God, wherfore fro than forthon they lived holyly and devoutly in our Lorde.'

Now King Oriant had ' made a Religion' at the hermitage where his son Helyas had been brought up; and thither, after recounting his adventures, the good Knight of the Swan betook himself, with a simple staff in his hand, and made himself a ' Religious.'

And close to the convent he caused to be built a castle like to that of Bouillon, and he called it Bouillon, and the forest'that was about it he called Dardayne, after the land that he had won from the Earl.

The English story here goes on to tell of the marriage of Eustace Earl of Boulogne and Ydain daughter of Helyas, and of the birth of her sons Godfrey, Baldwin, and Eustace ; and how that her mother, the Duchess of Bouillon, lamenting for the loss of her husband Helyas, sent messengers all over the world to find him ; and how that Ponce, one of these messengers, went to Jerusalem, and meeting there the Abbot Girarde of Saincteron, which is nigh to Bouillon, they determined as fellow-countrymen to return together. How they lose their way, and come to the castle of Bouillon *le restaure*, and are struck by the likeness to their own Bouillon ; how they inquire of the Curate, and hear who it was who built the castle and named the forest.

And how that they make themselves known to Emery and Helyas, and also to the King and Queen, who had come to live at the castle, and how they returned to their country, bearing a token from Helyas to his wife.

Then it tells how the Duchess and the Countess Ydain, whose sons were by this time adolescent, set forth to see their husband and father Helyas, and how they found him lying sick unto death, and how shortly thereafter ' he desceased in our lorde Jesu Chryst.'

How the ladies returned to Bouillon, and how the three noble brethren prepared themselves by a knightly education for the day when it should please God to give the kingdom of Jerusalem into the hands of Godfrey of Bouillon, the eldest born. 'And thus,' says Copland, ' endeth the life and myraculous hystory of the most noble and illustryous Helyas knight of the swanne, with the birth of the excellent knyght Godfrey of Boulyon, one of the nyne worthiest, and the last of the three crysten.'

The English romance, printed by Copland, is in some parts much fuller even than the French poem, going more into detail as to the wooing of King Oryens, and the cause of the enmity of Matabryne ; but here and there the French 'chanson' has details which Copland's book does not give ; such as the troublous adventures of

Helyas in his journey between Lilefort and Nimaye, and the acts and prowess of Godfrey, and his conquest of his kingdom ; but as to the legendary hero of the story, the Knight of the Swan, the tale of his deeds until his retirement from the world is mainly the same, in the English prose and in the French verse.

THE CASKET.

This curious work, of which I have before made mention, is an ancient ivory one, of 14th-century workmanship, now belonging to Mr William Gibbs of Tyntesfield, co. Somerset, and formerly to his wife's family, the Crawley-Boeveys, Baronets, of Flaxley Abbey, co. Gloucester. It is 8 inches long, 5⅝ deep, and 5½ inches high ; and in its thirty-six compartments it gives the history of the Knight of the Swan ; going no further than our poem, except that it depicts the capture of Matabryne's castle and the leave-taking and departure of Helyas. It is this last compartment that so nearly resembles the illumination at the head of the French poem.

I now proceed to describe the carvings in the several compartments, which are all of them remarkable for their accurate detail of arms and costume, and some groups, especially in Nos. 23 and 24, very spirited in their execution.

The top of the casket.

1. The King, Queen, and Matabryne on the wall. Mother and Twins below.
2. The King and the Queen in bed.
3. The King discovers that the Queen is with child.
4. The Queen asleep in bed : Matabryne carries off the children.
5. Matabryne delivers the children to Marcus.
6. Matabryne drowns the bitch in a well.
7. Matabryne presents the whelps to the King, who wrings his hands.
8. Marcus exposes the children in the forest.
9. Malkedras (?) thrusts the Queen into prison.
10. The hermit finds the children.
11. A hind suckles them ; and Malkedras finds them.
12. Malkedras tells Matabryne.

The front of the casket.

13. Malkedras takes the chains from the children's necks.

14. They fly away as swans.

15. Matabryne praises and caresses Malkedras.

16. Matabryne taunts the King, and gets leave to burn the Queen.

17. A soldier is leading the Queen to execution : she has fallen on her knees and is praying. See l. 90, note.

18. The King is on his throne as if to see the burning. Matabryne and a man in armour behind him, counselling him.

19. The angel appears to the hermit and the child.

20. The hermit and the child set forth on their way.

The left side of the casket.

21. The King on his throne ; the Queen presents the child as her champion, and Matabryne Malkedras as hers.

22. Combat between Helyas and Malkedras.

23. Helyas having slain Malkedras, bears away his head.

24. Flight of Matabryne.

The back of the casket.

25. Helyas presents the head of Malkedras to the King.

26. Reconciliation of King Oryens and Queen Beatrice.

27. The King and Queen embrace Helyas.

28. King Helyas with a kneeling figure before him. He seems to be giving something into his hand ; and perhaps it is a commission to a captain 'to prepaire a lytle hoste,' as Copland has it.

29. His army march against Matabryne.

30. They prepare to assault

31. The castle and its defenders.

32. Capture of Matabryne.

The right side of the casket.

33. Helyas recounts his adventures to his father and mother.

34. The burning of Matabryne.

35. The King and the Queen gazing

36. At Helyas departing in his ship alone, led by his brother the Swan.

The letter from Mr Dallaway, and extract of a letter from Mr Way in the note below, give the opinion of those antiquaries on the date and artistic value of this casket.[1]

[1] 'Mr Dallaway's respectful compliments to Sir Thomas Crawley, with the cabinet he has so long detained. He should have returned it with more satisfaction had he been able to discover the whole of the history represented, which is too complicated for him to unravel.

'Upon the upper compartment is evidently shown the well-known Legend of Isenbard, Earl of Altorf, and Irmentruda his wife, with her supernatural progeny.

'The two sons, who were preserved, were called Guelfo and Ghibelino, and their descendants were leaders of the factions by which the Italian States were distracted in the 12th century.

'He is of opinion that the remainder of their legendary story is described around the sides of the cabinet, and is not without hopes that, when he can meet with a very scarce collection of German novels, entitled "Camerarii Horæ Subcesivæ," it will furnish him with the whole of the detail.

'The armour and weapons of some of the figures are decidedly those of the 14th century, when elaborate carving was in very general use, and many Greek artists were encouraged ; which circumstance seems to establish the date of the specimen.

'The enclosed drawing Mr D. begs that Sir Thomas will accept, with many thanks, for the permission he has obtained to have it etched. He will take care that justice be done to it, and hopes that Sir T. will find room in his portfolio for some of the proof impressions.

'Jan. 5, 1793.

'Sir Thomas Crawley.'

———————

'*Wonham Manor,*
'*Reigate, Nov. 29, '60.*

'Dear Sir Martin,

'Your kindness in permitting me to bring home your curious ivory casket has, as I anticipated, enabled me to ascertain the whole of the subjects represented upon it. After much fruitless research, and showing the casket to several learned friends, I have at length got the right clue, and all difficulty ceases. The subjects are all from one romance, known as the "Knight of the Swan," and not found in any of the abstracts of middle-age romances, by Ellis, Dunlop, or the Italian writer Ferrario. It has, however, been published, but the volumes containing it are of very great rarity.

'I hope to send you an account of the romance, detailing the subjects as they occur on the casket. . . . . .

. . . .
. . . . . . I should almost suggest only to repair the broken portions of the metal bands as they exist, not to renew those which have been

ORIGIN OF THE ROMANCE.

Little or nothing can be added, on this head, to what Mr Thoms has collected in his preface to the Knight of the Swan ; and what I here write is chiefly drawn from that source.

Mr Utterson quotes Mr F. Cohen (Sir Francis Palgrave) for the opinion that the earliest form in which the story exists is in the Chronicle of Tongres, written by the Maitre de Guise, and incorporated in great part into the Mer des Hystoires. There is also, he says, an Icelandic Saga of Helis, the Knight of the Swan, in which he is called a son of Julius Cæsar ; and a similar legend is introduced into the German romance of *Lohengrin*, of which an edition was printed at Heidelberg as late as 1813. The story is still popular in Flanders, where a Chap-book, entitled De Ridder Met de Zwaen, was of frequent occurrence early in this century.

The immediate parent of the English prose romances on the subject appears to be the French folio printed in 1504, and entitled LA GENEALOGIE AVECQUES LES GESTES ET NOBLES FAITZ DARMES DU TRES PREUX ET RENOMME PRINCE GODEFFROY DE BOULION ET DE SES CHEUALEREUX FRERES BAUDOUIN ET EUSTACE, YSSUS & DESCENDUS DE LA TRES NOBLE & ILLUSTRE LIGNEE DU VERTUEUX CHEVALIER AU CYNE. AVECQUES AUSSI PLUSIEURS AUTRES CRONIQUES HYSTOIRES MIRACULEUSES ; TANT DU BON ROY SAINCT LOYS COMME DE PLUSIEURS AULTRES PUISSANS & VERTUEUX CHEVALIERS.

It was the first thirty-eight chapters of this work that were published in an English form by Robert Copland (which is the version edited by Mr Thoms) ; and Ames speaks of a translation published by Wynkyn de Worde, in 1512 ; but it is not now known to exist.

lost. . . . . It is to be considered that these metal bands are not original. The ivory dates from about 1380 ; the metal work about 1550. . . . .

'Believe me, very sincerely yours,

'ALBERT WAY.'

'Sir Martin Crawley-Boevey.'

Mr Way says in another letter that photographs had been taken of the casket. These I have never seen, but a set has been prepared expressly for this edition.

The tradition that the great Godfrey of Bouillon was descended from the Knight of the Swan, has always been a favourite one, and one of the most interesting stories in Otmar's Volksagen is founded on it. Nicolas de Klerc, in order to set right the common opinion in Flanders,

> Om dat van Brabant die Hertoghen
> Voormnels, dicke syn beloghen
> Alse dat sy quamen metten Swane
>
> [Forasmuch as the Dukes of Brabant
> have been heretofore much belied
> as that they came with a Swan],

professes to tell the truth about it in his Brabandshe Yeesten, written in 1318; and Marlaent refers to the same belief in his Spiegel Historiael.

On the other hand (through Godfrey, no doubt,) Robert Copland claims it as an honour for his patron, Edward Duke of Buckingham, that from the Knight of the Swan 'linially is dyscended my sayde Lorde.'

As to the portentous birth, which is the basis of the story, similar tales have been not unfrequently told. Amongst others there is one in which the house of Guelph is said to take its name from a like incident.

'Irmentrudes, wife of Isenbard Earl of Altorfe, accused a woman of adultery for bringing forth three children at a birth; adding withal that she was worthy to be sown in a sack, and thrown into the sea; and urged it very earnestly. It chanced in the year following, that she herself conceived, and in the absence of her husband, was delivered of twelve male children at one birth (though very little). But she, fearing the imputation and scandal she had formerly laid on the poor woman, and the law of like for like, caused her most trusty woman to make choice of one to be tendered to the father, and to drown all the residue in a neighbouring river. It fell out that the Earl Isenbard returning home, met this woman, demanding whither she went with her pail? who answered, " to drown a few baggage whelps in the river." The Earl would see them; and notwithstanding the woman's resistance, did so, and discovering the children, pressed her to tell the matter, which she also did; and he caused them all to be secretly nursed ; and, grown great, were brought home unto him, which he placed in an open hall with the son whom his wife had brought up, and soon known to be brethren by their likelihood in every respect. The Countess confessed the whole matter (moved with the sting of conscience), and was forgiven. In remembrance whereof, the illustrious race of the Welfes (whelps) got that name, and ever since hath kept it.'

Westcote (whose words I transcribe, as his book is a privately printed one (1845) from his MS. c. 1600) quotes this story from one Camerarius (he says) of Nuremberg, as a companion to a story of the wife of a peasant of Chumleigh, co. Devon, who had seven children at a birth, and whose husband, for fear of having to maintain so many mouths, resolves to drown them, and declares to the Countess of Devon, who meets him while on his errand, that they are but whelps. She rescues them and provides for them.

In French history we have a story somewhat analogous, in the efforts of the monks to separate Robert Capet and his wife, by persuading him that she had given birth to a monster.

The after part of the story of our book is the old one told with many variations from the time of the Shepherd David until now, of extreme youth, with the aid of the grace of God, vanquishing in battle the evil-doer, though a man of war from his youth.

THE VERSIFICATION OF THE POEM.

Coming now to the versification of the poem : I have thought it useful to analyse it so as to ascertain how far the author has kept himself to the rules of alliterative verse, as collected by Mr Skeat in his Essay on the subject prefixed to the 3rd volume of the Percy Folio.

The author seems to have contented himself with preserving generally the proper swing of his metre, the accentuated syllables marking it, in most cases, fairly well : but it often halts, the soft or unaccentuated syllables being awkwardly and too prodigally used, and the rime-letters very frequently falling on those syllables.

In many couplets the alliteration is utterly irregular, and in 10 couplets[1] I can discover none at all.

[1] 21, 34, 106, 225, 232, 334-6, 343, 367.

In 22 others[1] he has satisfied himself with a feeble sprinkling of the same letter through the verse without any regard to the loud syllables ; as

> 60. at a chamber dore as she forth sowȝte

sometimes also supplementing the weakness of one alliteration by adding a second in the same couplet ; as

> 241. that styked styffe in her BRestes · þat wolde þe qwene BRenne
>
> 287. A knyȝte kawȝte Hym by þe Honde · & ladde Hym of þe route.

The couplets in which there are but two rime-letters are very many ; no less than 143[2] out of the whole number of 370 ; and there are eight couplets[3] with four rime-letters.

The other variations from the established rule are: (a.) The occurrence of the chief letter on the second instead of the first loud syllable of the second line, which is found 64 times,[4] and of these 64, 29 ([5]) occur in couplets with but two rime-letters.

(b.) The occurrence of two rime-letters in the second line of the couplet, and but one in the first, in 37 couplets.[6]

(c.) The absence of the chief letter in the second limb of the couplet occurs 20 times.[7]

(d.) The rime-letters occur very often indeed upon unaccentuated or 'soft' syllables; so often, as to lead one to think that the author must have deemed his task fully done, if only there was any alliteration at all. The number is 72,[8] besides three in the next class.

---

[1] 13-4, 32, 49, 52, 60, 81, 96, 113, 132, 145, 158, 165, 185, 199, 210-1, 218, 272, 281-2, 351.

[2] 5, 6, 8, 10-1, 16, 24, 30-1, 40-1, 45-6, 54, 58, 63, 65, 75-6, 80, 82, 88, 90, 95, 99, 101, 103-5, 108, 110, 114-5, 120-1, 127-9, 137, 139, 142, 146, 149-50, 154-5, 160-2, 166-7, 172, 174, 181, 184, 189, 191-2, 195-6, 200-1, 208, 222, 227-9, 231, 240-1, 244, 247, 250-3, 256, 258, 264-5, 268-9, 271, 273, 280, 285-6, 290, 292, 294, 296, 299, 300, 302-6, 309, 314-6, 320-1, 323, 325, 327-8, 338, 353-4, 368-70.

[3] 2, 35, 42, 91, 152, 183, 239, 360.

[4] 1, 4, 20, 25-6, 30, 42, 53, 69, 70, 112, 136, 156, 173, 179, 183, 202, 212, 217, 226, 236, 239, 248, 261, 295, 310, 313, 317, 319, 324, 329, 331, 334, 355, 359. ([5]) 22, 37-8, 48, 56, 64, 86, 123, 140, 144, 164, 177, 182, 187-8, 190, 194, 203, 205-6, 207, 214, 236, 238, 246, 254, 308, 312, 363.

[6] 1, 12, 17, 23, 51, 78-9, 83-4, 107, 119, 135, 138, 141. 151, 159, 169, 170, 175, 198, 209, 223, 233-5, 237, 243, 255, 291, 293, 326, 340-2, 350, 356-7.

[7] 19, 50, 59, 67, 125, 153, 157, 163, 215, 219, 257, 259, 277, 279, 280, 332, 346-7, 352, 364.

[8] 2, 7, 23, 25-6, 28, 31, 35, 39, 40, 50-1, 66, 70, 73, 77, 79, 82, 102-3, 108-9,

(*c.*) Where the chief letter occurs in the initial catch of the second couplet.[1]

There are also *ten* couplets[2] with separate alliterations in each line, and

Seven,[3] in which there are no rime-letters in the first line.

And the couplets that appear to conform strictly to the canon of alliteration which provides that there shall be three rime-letters in each couplet, viz. two (sub-letters) in the accentuated syllables of the first line or limb of it, and one (the chief letter) on the first accentu-ated syllable of the second line, are 48 in number;[4] such as

> 92. Now Leve we þis Lady · in Langour & pyne
> 147. They sToden alle sTylle · for sTere þey ne durste

But of these 48, the alliteration is not always perfect, *w* having to do duty with words beginning with Oo (l. 29); *D* being once used as a rime-letter to *T* (l. 27), and the *G* in gladness being once considered mute, so as to rime the word with ' lay in langour' (l. 57).

The former editor draws attention to the existence of some rime-endings in this poem, but they seem to me to be accidental rather than intentional.

Mr Skeat enumerates them in his essay, and I set them down here, excepting those in lines 260-1, where he has been misled by the former editor's mistaking the long second *r* in *marre*, and reading it *marye;* and in 28, 29, where the editor has mistaken *leue* for *lene;*

12-13, *where* and *there*

31-32, *were* and *there*

158-159, *swyde* and *leyde.*   This is not a rime at all.

166-167, *juste* and *caste*

198-199, ⎫
350-351, ⎭ *swannes* and *cheynes.*   A very doubtful rime.

116, 118, 120, 126-8, 141, 143, 152, 156, 159, 161, 168-9, 175-6, 178, 180, 186, 191, 195, 202, 204, 209, 217, 220-1, 234-5, 250, 256, 261-2, 267, 270, 274, 278, 280, 283-4, 287-8, 292, 294, 337, 341, 343, 347-8, 357.

[1] 55, 75, 96.

[2] 44, 72, 85, 111, 216, 249, 266, 275, 330, 365.

[3] 117, 198, 245, 318, 345, 350, 362.

[4] 3, 9, 15, 18, 27, 29, 33, 36, 39, 43, 47, 57, 61-2, 71, 74, 87, 89, 91-4, 97-8, 100, 121, 131, 133-4, 147-8, 171, 193, 197, 213, 260, 263, 276, 297-8, 301, 307, 311, 322, 339, 349, 360-1, 366.

237-238, *were* and *mysfare ;*

and I may add 359-60, *made* and *bledde.*

But among these there are but three rimes which are at all perfect ; and it may be observed that in the 370 lines (from 200 to 570) of William of Palerne, which I have searched cursorily, there are as many :

As, 210, þat of horne ne of *hounde* · ne mizt he here *sowne*

   236-7, *telle* and *wille*

   337-8, *speche* and *riche*

   404, as euene as ani *wizt* · schuld attely bi *sizt*

   490-1, *wise* and *nyce*

   563-4, *newe* and *shewe ;*

so the rimes must, I think, be considered as an inadvertence on the part of the poet, and not as an intended embellishment.

CHARACTER OF THE MS.

The manuscript is neatly written in a handwriting of about 1460 ; and seemingly with few, if any, errors. At first sight the letter Thorn appears to be used indiscriminately for Th, but I find that it is *never* used at the beginning of a line, and *never* at the end of a word, whether it be written, for example, *serveth*, or *servethe*. The Th is used in proper names ; and the few other cases where it is found are, with one exception (thykke), where the sound occurs before the vowel *e.* Thus Sythen, Murther, Ferther, Therefore, and Beetheth, are thus spelt whenever they are found ; and Thefe is only once spelt þefe.

The ʒ is constantly used, representing *gh* in the middle of words and *y* at the beginning.

In most cases where we write *er* in our modern speech, and especially in word-endings, such as *after, water, together*, &c., the scribe uses a contraction representing *ur*, making the words *aftur, watur*, &c.

Where the double *l* is crossed (ꝉ), a final *e* has been assumed.

DATE AND DIALECT OF THE POEM.

The date of our poem in its present form appears to be the latter end of the 14th century; and the dialect in which it is written is Midland, and probably East Midland, as will be seen by the following observations.

The present indicative plurals of regular verbs end everywhere in -*en*. There appears to be an exception to this in l. 72, 'hem that it *deservethe;*' but 'hem' may either be miswritten for 'her;' or else perhaps it is used indeterminately, as 'they' and 'them' are sometimes used now-a-days.

It is not West Midland; for the 3rd sing. indic. almost universally ends in -*eth;* the only exceptions being '*lykes*' in l. 134; '*wendes*' in ll. 155 and 178; '*launces*' in l. 323, and '*formerknes*' in l. 362, though this last (see the note on the line) is a doubtful instance. Robert of Brunne also uses this termination in -*es;* but always, apparently, for the sake of the rime.

The second person sing. indic. ends in -*est;* excepting the word '*fyndes*' in l. 305. 'Thou *were*' is used in lines 236-7.

In many instances the *e* final is omitted in the past tense of weak verbs; as, delyvered, 155 and 178; graunted, 189 and 246. See also ll. 18, 24, 28, 39, 62, 91, 107, 108, 255, 275, 281, and 339.

There are some terminations in -*eth*, used instead of -*ed* for the perfect participles of regular verbs. See ll. 78, 175, 200, 209, 310.

The plurals of nouns end almost universally in -*es;* the only exceptions being *lond-is*, l. 16, *lyon-ys*, l. 214, and *bell-ys*, l. 272 (which are perhaps only variations made by the copyist); *dom-us*, l. 91; and *chylderen*, ll. 20 and 82.

Fader is uninflected in the possessive case, l. 203. The other genitives are in -*es*.

Some nouns of time and measure are uninflected in the plural; as ȝere, l. 89, 243 (we say now 'a two-*year*-old colt'), and *myle*, l. 95 (we say now 'it is a *two-mile* course').

Of the personal pronouns—

I is always used, and not *Ic*.

All people alike, king and peasant, *Thou* and *Thee* one another, without the distinction of rank, such as is shown in William of Palerne, by the use of *Ye* and *You*. In one instance, l. 26, the King addresses the Queen as *Ye*. *Hym* is the objective singular, and *Hem* (in one instance *Ham*, probably for þam—a Northern form) the plural : *Them* is never used.

She is the 3rd person fem. nominative, and *Here* or *Her* objective, the latter being used 8 times in the poem, and the former 9.

Hit and *It* are used about equally, the latter rather more frequently. *They* is always used in the plural.

The possessive pronoun of the 3rd person feminine, is *Her* or *Here*. In the plural of all genders it is *Here*, and once *Her*.

The negative form of the verb To Be is once used in *Nere* = ne were, l. 3.

The imperfect participles end always in *-ynge*.

This is contrary to early Midland usage, and seems to show that the dialect here employed must have been spoken in the Southern part of the East Midland district, *-inge* being a Southern form, though it is used in another East Midland book, 'Body and Soul,' l. 396 [brennynge], and by Robert of Brunne 'Handlyng Synne;' and by Chaucer. But as the peculiarities of each dialect were no doubt always understood by the neighbours on the borders of the several districts, and by degrees became naturalized beyond their ancient limits; so probably at the time when the Cheualere Assigne was written, the Southern and Midland dialects at least were beginning to blend and form a common language.

One peculiarity in this author's style is a strange mixing of past and present tenses ; i. e. in the same sentence he constantly, as does also Chaucer sometimes, uses the historical present, and the perfect. Thus in l. 229,

'The chylde *stryketh* hym to, & *toke* hym by þe brydelle.'

See also lines 63, 115-16, 151, 155, 173, 178, 190, 221, 267, 332, 341, 355, 361-2, and 365.

Mr Morris writes, 'The Dialect in its *present form* is East Midland. But as we do not find [other] East Midland writers adopting alliterative measure in the 14th century, I am inclined to think that the original English text was written in the N. or N.W. of England, and that the present copy is a mere modified transcript. This theory accounts for the *es's* in the 3rd person [sing.], which are not required for the rime, and may be forms belonging to the earlier copy, and unaltered by the later scribe.'

I have to thank Mr Morris, Mr Skeat, and Mr Furnivall for their kind suggestions during the progress of my work, and I must make also my acknowledgments to Mr Brock for his faultless transcript.

Although, therefore, I suppose that, from their uncertain character, the dialect or grammatical peculiarities of this poem are not of any particular value in the history of the language, yet as it is at any rate a contribution to that history, and as I think that whatever is worth doing at all, is worth doing thoroughly, I have made the Glossary as copious and accurate as I could. Besides, there is some spirit and vigour in the Poem itself; and I hope the reading of the little book may be as entertaining to the members of the Early English Text Society, as the editing of it has been to me.

H. H. G.

POSTSCRIPT TO THE PREFACE

OF THE

Chevelere Assigne.

IN the foregoing Preface I have given a short account of the story told in the cycle of Lays, of which the "Chevalier Assigne" (Helyas) forms a part, and to which it gives a name, but it may be well that I should describe more precisely the component parts of the Cycle in question, and fix the place which it holds in the list of Rhapsodies commemorating the deeds of the ancient heroes of romance.

These songs of the Troubadours—the Homers of the Middle Ages—were called *Chansons de Geste* (historic songs), and told of the exploits of Charlemagne and his mighty men, of William of Orange (otherwise called William with the Short Nose), of the four sons of Aymon; of Arthur and his knights; of Jerusalem and its fortunes, and of the heroes who fought in the Crusades for its recovery from the enemies of the Faith.

The Lives or Acts of the various heroes commemorated form severally branches of the principal epic cycle under which they are ranged, whether of Charlemagne, of the Round Table, or of that with which we are here concerned, and which was called "the Cycle of the knight of the Swan," or else "the Cycle of Godfrey of Boulogne." Under this latter cycle are grouped five lays, properly belonging to it, forming what we may call a Godofrediad, since it is all, or almost all, written to Godfrey's glory, beginning with the miraculous birth of his ancestor Helyas, and ending with his crowning deed, the capture of Jerusalem.

These five lays are,

I. The Chanson d'Antioche, treating of the Voyage of Peter the hermit, the entry of the Crusaders into Palestine, and the conquest of Antioch. It is the earliest in point of composition, and appears to have been the germ and nucleus of the other members of the cycle, as well as a model for the songs of other Troubadours. From their writings we gather that it was current early in the 12th century. To the Chevalier William of Bechada, who wrote before 1137, to William, Count of Poitiers, and to Richard the pilgrim, himself present at the first Crusade, has the honour of its composition been attributed; but we know it only in the more modern form given to it by the Troubadour Graindor of Douai in 1268. It was edited in 1848, by M. Paulin Paris.

II. The Chanson de Jerusalem, describing the conquest of the Holy City, was founded on the lay of Richard the pilgrim; but has come down to us only in the revision of Graindor (published by M. Hippeau in 1868), who in arranging anew this and the preceding Geste, incorporated with them

III. The Lay of the Captives (*Chetifs*), a work of a later period in the same century, but founded, so M. Paulin Paris thinks, on a Chanson of William IX, Count of Poitiers, who returned to his country in 1102, one of the few survivors of a disastrous expedition to the East, of which he was the leader after the entry of the crusaders into Jerusalem.

IV. The Lay of Helyas, being the story of the Knight of the Swan himself; the beginning of which, as quoted below, shows that this branch at least of the cycle was of later date than the cycle of Arthur. It appears to have been written about 1190.

V. Les Enfances de Godeffroy, the earlier form of which seems to have been written by a nameless Troubadour in the first part of the 12th century; and the later version by one Renaud or Renax, in the later years of the same, or early in the succeeding, century.

The French poem to which I referred in the Preface, as contained in the "Shrewsbury book" (Royal. 15 E vj in the British Museum), appears to be an amalgamation into one Chanson of all the five branches of this cycle.

It differs very considerably from the version of the Chanson extant in the MSS. consulted by M. Paris, as is evident from a comparison of the British Museum MS. with the extracts given by him in the 22nd volume of the *Histoire Litteraire de la France*. Many lines are the same, many slightly altered, and many lines, and even long passages, are omitted in one and find a place in the other. These variations no doubt arise from the handing down the lays from bard to bard, by oral tradition in a great measure ; each singer drawing from his imagination to supply any lack in his memory ; and each probably, by dictation to some scribe, perpetuating his variations, whether of matter or dialect, in his own province or neighbourhood.

Take, for example, the first five lines of the poem (after the two quoted on p. ii. in the note), which in the Paris MS. stand as

> Teus i a qui vous cantent de la Reonde Table,
> Des manteaux anjoulés, de samis et de sable ;
> Mais jou ne vous voel dire ne mensonge ne fable.
> En escrist la fist la bone dame Orable
> Dedens les murs d'Orange la fort cité mirable ;

and in the London MS. as

> Telȝ y a qui nous chantent de la Ronde table,
> Des manteaulx angolés, de samin et de sable ;
> Mais je ne vous diray ne menconge ne flabe ; [*sic*]
> Quer il est en ystoire, cest chose veritable,
> En escript le fist mettre la bonne dame orable.

Again, the description of the birth of the children occupies but four lines in the MS. quoted by M. Paris :

> Au naistre des enfans set fées y avoit
> Qui les enfans faerent, si com lor aveuroit
> Et quant l'uns des enfans après l'autre nascoit
> Au col une caïne de blanc argent avoit ;

but the Shrewsbury book gives eight to them and Matabrune :

> Au naistre des enfans nulle femme ny avoit
> Fors une vielle dame qui eu Dieu pou creoit
> Mere estoit au *Seigneur*, la royne fort hayoit,
> A amasser avoir tout son penser estoit.
> La dame se delivre a paine et a destroit ;
> L'un enfant à pres lautre si com dieu le voulloit,

> Si com l'un enfant à pres lautre naissoit,
> Au col une chaine de fin argent avoit.

The account of the sorrowful leavetaking of Helyas and his Beatrice is thus ended in the Paris and London MS. respectively—

> Là plorent vavassor et prince et castelain,
> Oneques n'en ot à Blaives si grant duel por Audain,
> Quant fut morte de duel por son cousin germain.
>
> Lors pleurent prevost et chastelain,
> Dames et pucelle, noble; et vilain ;
> Plus de c se pasmerent sur le terrain.

The name Helyas (in its various forms of Helias, Helius, Helis or Elis, Elias, and Salvius) is derived by Mr Baring-Gould from the Keltic Ala, Eala, Ealadh, a Swan. See his " Curious Myths of the Middle Ages" (2nd Series, 1868), which contains an interesting treatise on the Legend of the Knight of the Swan.

In further illustration of my subject I will mention that the museum of the *Maison de Cluny* at Paris contains an ivory casket, the carvings on which represent a part of the story of our book. According to M. Francisque Michel, its date is of the end of the 13th or beginning of the 14th century. It is not nearly so full in its details as the Tyntesfield casket, but is interesting as giving additional evidence of the popularity of the legend of the CHEVALIER AU CYGNE.

H. H. GIBBS.

2 *Sept.*, 1870.

.;. CHEUELERE .;. ASSIGNE .;.

[*Cotton MS. Caligula* A. ii., *fol.* 125 *b.*]

¶ Alle weldynge god · whenne it is his wylle,
Wele he wereth his · werke with his owne honde :
For ofte harmes were hente · þat helpe we ne myȝte ;
Nere þe hyȝnes of hym · þat lengeth in heuene.　　4
For this I saye by a lorde · was lente in an yle,
That was kalled lyor · a londe by hym selfe.
The kynge hette oryens · as þe book tellethe ;
And his qwene bewtrys · þat bryȝt was & shene :　　8
¶ His moder hyȝte Matabryne · þat made moche sorwe ;
For she sette her affye · in Sathanas of helle.
This was chefe of þe kynde · of cheualere assygne ;
And whenne þey sholde in-to a place · it seyth fulle
　　wele where,　　　　　　　　　　　　　　12
Sythen aftur his lykynge · dwellede he þere,
Withe his owne qwene · þat he loue myȝte :
But alle in langour he laye · for lofe of here one,
That he hadde no chylde · to cheuenne his londis ;　　16
¶ But to be lordeles of his · whenne he þe lyf lafte :
And þat honged in his herte · I heete þe for sothe.

God Almighty guards us,

as we see by the story of King Oryens,

and Beatrice his queen, and his mother Matabryne.

He had no child to succeed him, which was a grief.

Line 5. See note on l. 23.
6. lyor. In the French poem it is *Lilefort*, and in Copland also.
7—9. The King is called *Oriant* in the French version, and the Queen *Bietrix*, and the King's mother *Matebrune*.

11. 'This' must mean 'this King.'
12. I cannot make sense of this line. 'Sholde' = should go, and 'it' means the book.
18. honged in his herte = weighed upon his mind.

The King and the Queen, talking on the wall, see beneath them a woman with her twins,

As þey wente vp-on a walle · pleynge hem one,
Bothe þe kynge & þe qwene · hem selfen to-gedere : 20
The kynge loked a-downe · & by-helde vnder,
And sey3 a pore womman · at þe 3ate Sytte,
Withe two chylderen her by-fore · were borne at a
   byrthe ;

whereat he weeps.

And he turned hym þenne · & teres lette he falle.   24
¶ Sythen sykede he on-hy3e · & to þe qwene sayde,
'Se 3e þe 3onder pore womman · how þat she is pyned
Withe twynlenges two · & þat dare I my hedde wedde.'

The Queen says she disbelieves in twins. Each must have a father.

The qwene nykked hym with nay · & seyde 'it is not
   to leue :   28
Oon manne for oon chylde · & two wymmen for
   tweyne ;
Or ellis hit were vnsemelye þynge · as me wolde þenke,
But eche chylde hadde a fader · how manye so þer
   were.'

The King rebukes her,

The kynge rebukede here for her worþes ry3te þere ; 32
¶ And whenne it drow3 towarde þe ny3te · þey wenten
   to bedde ;

and at night begets on her reasonably many children,

He getto on here þat same ny3te · resonabullye manye.
The kynge was witty · whenne he wysste her with
   chylde,
And þankede lowely our lorde · of his loue & his
   sonde.   36

19. walle. The French has 'tour.'
23. Chaucer frequently omits the relative, as is done here.
26. 'is pyned' must mean 'has travailed,' or been in pain.
28. it is not to leue. The edition of 1820 has leue. In the French it is rous parlez de neant.
29. This means, 'One man can beget but one child, nor can one woman have more than one at a time by the same man. Two honestly-begotten children must needs have two mothers.' Twins were once thought to reflect on the mother's chastity.
The French poem has

Sa deux hommes ne sest lirree charnellement.
31. how manye so = howso[ever] many.
32. ry3te there = On the spot.
33 & 37. drow3 and drow3e. 'The correct form is drow.'—R. Morris.
34. He gette, &c. It is printed gotte in the Roxb. ed., but the word is plainly gette in the MS. The French has

Engendra lo seigneur en la dame raillant
vij enfans celle nuit en ung engendrement.

But whenne it drowȝe to þe tyme · she shulde be de-
  lyuered,
Ther moste no womman come her nere · but she þat
  was cursed,
His moder matabryne · þat cawsed moche sorowe ;
For she thowȝte to do þat byrthe · to a fowle ende. 40
¶ Whenne god wolde þey were borne · þenne browȝte
  she to honde
Sex semelye sonnes · & a dowȝter þe seueneth,   to wit, six sons
                                                 and a daughter,

.;. MATABRYNE. .;.   [Fol. 126.]

Alle safe & alle sounde · & a seluer cheyne   with silver chains
Eche on of hem hadde · a-bowte his swete swyre. 44 about their necks.
And she lefte hem out · & leyde hem in a cowche ;
And þenne she sente aftur a man · þat markus was But Matabryne
  called,   sends for her man
                                                   Marcus,
That hadde serued her-seluen · skylfully longe :
He was trewe of his feyth · & loth for to tryfulle ; 48
¶ She knewe hym for swych · & triste hym þe better ;
And seyde, ' þou moste kepe counselle · & helpe what
  þou may :
The fyrste grymme watur · þat þou to comeste,   51 and bids him
Looke þou caste hem þer-In · & lete hym forthe slyppe : drown the
                                                     children.
Sythen seche to þe courte · as þou nowȝte hadde sene,
And þou shalt lyke fulle wele · yf þou may lyfe aftur.'

39. ' þat cawsed moche sorowe.'
These words, and ' the cursede man in
his feyth,' are, like the Homeric ποδας
ωκυς and ποιμενα λαων, applied as a
sort of verse-tag to fill up the line, and
serve as constant epithets respectively
to Matabryne and Malkedras.
40. do.. to a fowle ende. See l. 138.
As in Shakespere, Much Ado about
Nothing, V. 3 : ' Done to death with
slanderous tongues.'
45. lefte = lifted.
46. Markus, called Marques and
Marcon in the French poem.
49. knewe, should be knew ; the e
is superfluous ; but it is so in the MS.

49. swych. Wrongly printed snyth
in the Roxb. ed.
triste. Wrongly printed tristed, in
the same, moste ; the e is superfluous.
50. kepe counselle = be secret.
52. hym for hem.
53. seche = betake thyself. Comp.
Ezekiel xiv. 10, ' him that seeketh
unto him.'
54. lyke full wele = be well-liking
= prosper. Comp. ' fat and well-liking,' Ps. xcii. 13 ; ' worse-liking,' Daniel
i. 10. ' I believe the original con-
struction was, " And it shal like þe ful
wel " = and it shall please thee full
well. See l. 134.'—R. Morris.

Whenne he herde þat tale · hym rewede þe tyme;

She marginal: *Marcus grieves, but dares not disobey.*

But he durste not werne · what þe qwene wolde.   56

¶ The kynge lay in langour · sum gladdenes to here;

But þe fyrste tale þat he herde · were tydynges febulle,

Whenne his moder matabryne · browʒte hym tydynge.

At a chamber dore · as she forthe sowʒte,   60

She takes seven whelps,

Seuenne whelpes she sawe · sowkynge þe damme,

And she kawʒte out a knyfe · & kylled þe bycche;

She caste her þenne in a pytte · & takethe þe welpes,

And sythen come byfore þe kynge · & vp on-hyʒe she seyde,   64

and shows 'em to the King as the Queen's off-spring, and bids him have her burnt.

¶ 'Sone paye þe with þy qwene · & se of her berthe.'

Thenne syketh þe kynge · & gynnythe to morne,

And wente wele it were sothe · alle þat she seyde.

Thenne she seyde, 'lette brenne her a-none · for þat is þe beste.'   68

He refuses.

'Dame, she is my wedded wyfe · fulle trewe as I wene,

As I haue holde her er þis · our lorde so me helpe!'

She vituperates.

'A, kowarde of kynde,' quod she · '& combred wrecche!

Wolt þou werne wrake · to hem þat hit deserueth?'

He says, 'Stow her where thou wilt, so that I see it not.'

¶ 'Dame, þanne take here þy selfe · & sette her wher þe lykethe,   73

So þat I se hit noʒte · what may I seye elles?'

Thenne she wente her forthe · þat god shalle confounde,

She falls foul of the Queen,

To þat febulle þer she laye · & felly she bygynnethe,   76

And seyde, 'a-ryse wrecched qwene · & reste þe her no lengur;

Thow hast by-gylethe my sone · it shalle þe werke sorowe:

Bothe howndes & men · haue hadde þe a wylle:

Thow shalt to prisoun fyrste · & be brente aftur.'   80

---

60. sowʒte. See note on l. 53.
64. come. The correct form is *com*.
on-hyʒe = aloud.
68. lette brenne her = have her burnt.
72. deserueth. As to this termina-

tion in -*eth*, see Preface, p. xvi.
75. See note on l. 190.
78. by-gylethe. The final *e* is un-necessary; but there is a contraction representing it in the MS.

¶ Thenne shrykede þe ȝonge qwene · & vp on hyȝ   *and, in spite of her moans,*
cryethe,

' A, lady,' sho seyde · ' where ar my lefe chylderen ? '

Whenne she myssede hem þer · grete mone she made.

By þat come tytlye · tyrauntes tweyne,   84

And by þe byddynge of matabryne · a-non þey her hente,

And in a dymme prysoun · þey slongen here deepe,   *[Fol. 126 b.] has her thrown*

And leyde a lokke on þe dore · & leuen here þere : 87   *into prison,*

Mete þey caste here a-downe · & more god sendethe.   *where she lies eleven years.*

¶ And þus þe lady lynede þere · elleuen ȝere,

And mony a fayre orysoun · vn-to þe fader made,

That saued Susanne fro sorowefulle domus · [her] to   *But God, who saved Susanna, hears her prayer also.*
saue als.

Now lene we þis lady in langour & pyne,   92

And turne aȝeyne to our tale · towarde þese chylderen,

And to þe man markus · þat murther hem sholde ;

How he wente þorow a foreste · fowre longe myle,   *Marcus takes the children to drown them.*

Thylle he come to a watur · þer he hem shulde in
drowne ;   96

¶ And þer he keste vp þe clothe · to knowe hem bettur,   *But they look on him in lovely wise,*

And þey ley & lowȝe on hym · louelye alle at ones :

' He þat lendethe wit,' quod he · ' leyne me wyth sorowe,   *and he won't,*

If I drowne ȝou to day · thowghe my deth be nyȝe.' 100

Thenne he leyde hem adowne · lappedde in þe mantelle,   *but leaves them all wrapped in a mantle, and commends them to Christ.*

And lappede hem, & hylyde hem · & hadde moche
rewthe,

That swyche a barmeteme as þat · shulde so be-tyde.

Thenne he takethe hem to criste · & aȝeyne turnethe. 104

---

81. See note on l. 64.

84. By þat = by that time, then.

tyrauntes. The French poem has *Sers* (serfs).

86. slongen. Roxb. ed. has *flongen*, which is an error of transcription.

90. This particular orison, with Susanna for its example, finds a place in the French poem, not at this point, but during the procession from the city to the place of burning, Mata-

bryne's remark thereon being ' *ça ne vault vng bouton.*'

91. domus. This *might* be a mis-writing for ' *dom* (= doom) *us*,' as the former edition reads it ; but it is, no doubt, a plural in *us*, the word *her* having slipped out.

99. wit. Wrongly printed *wt* in the former edition.

103. swyche. See note on l. 49.

¶ But sone þe mantelle was vn-do · wit*h* mengynge of
    her legges ;

They cryedde vp on-hyȝe · wit*h* a dolefulle steuenne,

They chynered for colde · as cheuerynge chyldreñ,

A hermit hears them sob, They ȝoskened, & cryde out · & þut a man herde,   108

An holy hermyte was by · & towarde hem comethe :

Whe*n*ne he come by-tore hem · on knees þe*n*ne he felle,

and cries to Christ for suc-cour; And cryede ofte vpon cryste · for so*m*me soko*ur* hym
    to sende,

If any lyfe were hem lente · in þis worlde leng*ur*.   112

a hind comes and suckles them ; ¶ Thenne an hynde kome fro þe woode · rennynge fulle
    swyfte,

And felle be-fore hem adowñe · þey drowȝe to þe
    pappes ;

The heremyte prowde was þer-of · & putte hem to
    sowke :

and the hermit takes them home and tends them. Sethen taketh he hem vp · & þe hynde folowethe,   116

And she kepte hem þere · whylle our lorde wolde.

Thus he noryscheth hem vp · & criste hem helpe send-
    ethe.

Of sadde leues of þe wode · wrowȝte he hem wedes.

Malkedras the Forester passes and sees them, Malkedras þe fostere · þe fende mote hym haue,   120

¶ That cursedde man for his feythe · he come þer þey
    wereñ,

And was ware in his syȝte · syker of þe chyldren ;

He tu*r*nede aȝeyn to þe courte · & tolde of þe chaunce,

tells Matabryne, And menede byfore matabryne · how mony þer were. 124

' And more meruecyle þe*n*ne þat · Dame, a seluere cheyne

Eche on of hem hath · abowte here swyre.'

She seyde, ' holde þy wordes in chaste · þat none skape
    ferther ;

I wylle soone aske hym · þat hath me betrayed.'   128

---

119. sadde leues of þe wode.   Fr. *feuilles de loriers.*

120. Malkedras is called in the French MS. *Malquarrez* and *Mauquarre.*

124. menede.   Wrongly printed *meuede* in the Roxb. ed.

127. holde thy wordes in chaste = be silent.

¶ Thenne she sente aftur markus · þat murther hem who questions
  sholde ;

And askede hym, in good feythe · what felle of þe
  chyldren :

Whenne she hym asked hadde · he seyde, 'here þe
  sothe ;

Dame, on a ryueres banke · lapped in my mantelle, 132
I lafte hem lyynge there · leue þou for sothe :
I my3te not drowne hem for dole · do what þe lykes.'
Thenne she made here alle preste · & (putt) out bothe
  hys yen.

Moche mone was therfore · but no man wyte moste. 136

¶ 'Wende þou a3eyne malkedras · & gete me þe cheynes,
And withe þe dynte of þy swerde · do hem to dethe ;
And I shalle do þe swych a turne · & þou þe tyte hy3e,
That þe shalle lyke ry3te wele · þe terme of þy lyue.' 140
Thenne þe hatefulle thefe · hyed hym fulle faste,
The cursede man in his feythe · come þer þey were.

By þenne was þe hermyte go in-to þe wode · & on of
  þe childreñ,

For to seke mete · for þe other sex, 144

¶ Whyles þe cursed man · asseylde þe other :
And he out withe his swerde · & smote of þe cheynes.
They stoden alle stylle · for stere þey ne durste ;
And whenne þe cheynes felle hem fro · þey floweñ vp
  swannes 148

To þe ryuere by-syde · withe a rewfulle steuenne.
And he takethe vp þe cheynes · & to þe cowrte
  turnethe,

And come by-fore þe qwene · & here hem bytakethe :
Thenne she toke hem in honde · & heelde ham fulle
  stylle ; 152

¶ She sente aftur a golde-smy3te · to forge here a cowpe ;

Marginal notes (right column):
who questions
Marcus,

and, hearing the
truth, has his
eyes put out ;

sends Malkedras
to take the chains,
and slay the
children.

He finds but six,
one being away
with the hermit.

He smites off the
chains ; and the
children change
into swans.

---

133. leue. Wrongly printed *lene* in of the MS. by the original scribe.
the edition of 1820.   138. do. See note on l. 40.
  135. The Roxb. ed. omits *putt*, 140. See note on l. 54.
which has been added in the margin

The old Queen
gives the chains
to a goldsmith to
make a cup of.

And whenne þe man was comen · þenne was þe qwene
   blythe,

And delyuered hym his weyȝtes · & he from cowrte
   wendes :

She badde þe wesselle were made · vpoñ alle wyse : 156

The goldesmyȝth goothe & beetheth hym a fyre · &
   brekethe a cheyne,

One chain mul-
tiplies so in the
melting-pot, that
half of one
suffices.

And it wexeth in hys honde · & multyplyethe swyde :

He toke þat oþur fyue · & fro þe fyer hem leyde,

And made hollye þe cuppe · of haluendelle þe sixte. 160

¶ And whenne it drowȝe to þe nyȝte · he wendethe to
   bedde,

The goldsmith
tells his wife, and
asks her counsel.

And thus he seythe to his wyfe · in sawe as I telle.

'The olde qwene at þe courte · hathe me bytaken

Six cheynes in honde · & wolde haue a cowpe ;   164

And I breke me a cheyne · & halfe leyde in þe fyer,

And it wexedde in my honde · & wellede so faste,

That I toke þe oþur fyve · & fro þe fyer caste,

And haue made hollye þe cuppe · of haluendele þe
   sixte.'   168

She says, ' Keep
the rest ! The
Queen has full
weight. What
would she have
more ? '
[Fol. 127 b.]

¶ ' I rede þe,' quod his wyfe · ' to holden hem stylle ;

Hit is þorowe þe werke of god · or þey be wronge
   wonneñ ;

For whenne here mesure is made · what may she aske
   more ? '   171

And he dedde as she badde · & buskede hym at morwe ;

He gives the old
Queen the cup
and the half
chain.

He come by-fore þe qwene · & bytaketh here þe cowpe,

And she toke it in honde · & kepte hit fulle clene.

' Nowe lefte ther ony ouur vn-werkethe · by þe better
   trowthe ? '

And he recheth her forth · halueñdele a cheyne : 176

---

162. The conversation between the
goldsmith and his wife is much longer
and more dramatic in our poem than
in the French.

170. þorowe. Wrongly printed *Thòwe*
in the Roxb. ed.

170. wronge wonnen=wrongly (i. e.
wrongfully) acquired.

176. recheth. Misprinted *recketh*.
forth. Misprinted *ferth* in the
Roxb. ed.

¶ And she raw3te hit hym a3eyne · & seyde she ne
   row3te ;
She gives him the half chain and his pay.

But delyuered hym his scruyse · & he out of cowrte
   wendes.

'The curteynesse of criste,' quod she · 'be with þese
   oþur cheynes !   179

They be delyuered out of þis worlde · were þe moder eke,

Thenne hadde I þis londe · hollye to myne wylle :

Now alle wyles shalle fayle · but I here dethe werke.'

At morn she come byfore þe kynge · & by ganne fulle
   keene ;   183
She scolds the King for leaving his Queen so long unburnt,

' Moche of þis worlde sonne · wondrethe on þe aþone,

¶ That thy qwene is vnbrente · so meruelows longe,

That hath serued þe dethe · if þou here dome wyste :

Lette sommene þy folke · vpon eche a syde,
and bids him summon his folk.

That þey bene at þy sy3te · þe .xj. day assygned.' 188

And he here graunted þat · withe a grymme herte ;
He grieves ; but grants it.

And she wendeth here adowñ · & lette hem a-none
   warne.

The ny3te byfore þe day · þat þe lady shulde brenne,
The night before the burning

An Angelle come to þe hermyte · & askede if he slepte :
comes an angel to the hermit.

¶ The angelle seyde, 'criste sendeth þe worde · of þese
   six chyldreñ ;   193

And for þe sauynge of hem · þanke þou haste seruethe :

They were þe kynges Oriens · wytte þou for sothe,

179. *'Puis dist entre ses dens assez bassetement*
Bien suis de ceulx delivre alez sont voirement
Se leur mere estoit arse ne me chauldroit neant.
And then,' she continues, 'by my enchantments I will cause that my son never marries again, and so I shall have all the land at my command.'

186. serued. In the Roxb. ed. this is erroneously printed dyserved.
if thou here dome wyste = if thou knewest what her sentence ought to be.
190. wendeth here. 'wend' is here used reflexively as 'went' is in l. 75,

and 'hy3e' in l. 141, after the French s'en alla. Comp. Shaksp. 2 Gent. of Ver. IV. 4 : 'I .. goes me to the fellow.' The phrase in the text seems to make it more probable that this me is the personal, and not the indeterminate pronoun.
194. þanke þou haste seruethe = thou hast deserved thanks. The final e is too much. See note on l. 78.
195. They were the kynges Oriens = They were [the children] of the King Oriens. This expression is not unlike that in Wm. of Palerne, l. 5437 : þemperours moder William.

Tells him that the six swan-children are sons of Oryens and Beatrice.

By his wyfe Betryce · she bere hem at ones,   196

For a worde on þe walle · þat she wronge seyde;

And ȝonder in þe ryuer · swymmen þey swannes;

Sythen Malkedras þe forsworn þefe · byrafte hem her
    cheynes:

But that Christ formed the other child to fight for his mother.

And criste hath formeth þis chylde · to fyȝte for his
    moder.'   200

¶ 'Oo-lyuynge god þat dwellest in heuene' · quod þe
    hermyte þanne,

'How can this be?'

'How sholde he serue for suche a þynge · þat neuer
    none syȝe?'

'Take him to Court and have him christened Enyas.'

'Go brynge hym to his fader courte · & loke þat he be
    cristened;   203

And kalle hym Enyas to name · for awȝte þat may be-falle,

Ryȝte by þe mydday · to redresse his moder;

For goddes wylle moste be fulfylde · & þou most forthe
    wende.'

The heremyte wakynge lay · & thowȝte on his wordes:

Soone whenne þe day come · to þe chylde he seyde,   208

The hermit tells the child what he is to do, what a mother is,
[Fol. 128.]

¶ 'Criste hath formeth þe sone · to fyȝte for þy moder.'

He asskede hymm þanne · what was a moder.

'A womman þat bare þe to man · sonne, & of her reredde:'

'ȝe, kanste þou, fader, enforme me · how þat I shalle
    fyȝte?'   212

'Vpon a hors,' seyde þe heremyte · 'as I haue herde seye.'

---

201. Oo. Wrongly printed *To* in the former edition. Oo-lyuynge = everliving.

202. þynge. Wrongly printed ȝnge in the former edition.

204. Enyas; not *Ænyas*, as in the old edition. The French poem has *Elyas* or *Helyas*, which latter is the name given him in the English prose Romance.

A line seems to be omitted between 204 and 205, such as

'Let hym cair to þe court · þer þe
  kynge dwellethe.'

210. The conversation between the hermit and the child is more full in the English than in the French poem.

211. A very cramped line. 'A woman that bare thee to man, [my] son; and [thou wast] by her reared.'

'It means, "bare thee so that thou becamest a man." Such is the regular idiom; [God] *wrouȝt me to man* = formed thee so that thou becamest a man, fashioned thee in man's shape; occurs in Piers Plowman, A. Pass. i. l. 80.'—W. W. S.

'*Beau filz cest une femme quen ses
  flans te porta.*'

'What beste is þat?' quod þe chylde · 'lyonys wylde? and what a horse, on which he is to fight.
Or elles wode? or watur' · quod þe chylde þanne.

'I seyȝe neuur none,' quod þe hermyte · 'but by þe mater
    of bokes :   216

¶ They seyn he hath a feyre hedde · & fowre lymes hye ;
And also he is a frely beeste · for-thy he man seructhe.'

'Go we forthe, fader,' quod þe childe 'vpon goddes halfe!' The child is willing, and they go forth on their way.
The grypte eyþur a staffe in here honde · & on here wey
    strawȝte.   220

Whenne þe heremyte hym lafte · an angelle hym suwethe, The hermit leaves the child, and an angel goes with him and counsels him.
Euur to rede þe chylde · vpon his ryȝte sholder.
Thenne he seeth in a felde · folke gaderynge faste, The child sees a great crowd and a fire kindled in a field,
And a hyȝ fyre was þer bette · þat þe qwene sholde in
    brenne,   224

¶ And noyse was in þe cyte · felly lowde, and a great troop bringing the Queen from the city.
With trumpes & tabers · whenne þey here vp token ;
The olde qwene at here bakke · betynge fulle faste ;
The kynge come rydynge a-fore · a forlonge & more ; 228 The King rides in front.
The chylde stryketh hym to · & toke hym by þe brydelle : 'Who art thou? and who are these?' quoth the child.
'What man arte þou?' quod þe chylde · '& who is þat
    þe svethe?'

215. Or else [a] wood[-beast], or [a] water[-beast] ?
219. Comp. William of Palerne, l. 2803, 'Go we now on goddes halve.'
220. The grypte eyþur = They each seized.
221. suwethe. The Roxb. editor has mistaken this for *seemeth*.
221-2. rede. Here we find *ride* in the former edition ; but besides that it is not so written, the French original shows that it must be as in the text. This incident of the angel does not find its place here, in the French poem. There, it is when the child accosts the King that the author says,—
    *Homme fol et sauvaige a merveilles
      sembloit
    Lange a dieu le pere sur lespaule
      seoit
    Que ce quil devoit dire trop bien lui
      enseignoit.*

224. brenne. The final *e* is illegible, being obliterated by a blot of ink.
bette. Comp. Sir Aldingar, l. 53 (Percy folio, vol. i, p. 168), 'And fayre fyer there shalbe *bette*.'
227. *A tant est Matebrune qui
    a-maine a grant cris
Batant la bonne dame qui eust nom
    Bietrix.*
230. Here in the French poem follows,
             ' Le roy . . .
*Voulentiers en eust ris mais trop
    dolent estoit.'*
He then asks the child what his own name is ; and he answers that he has no name, except that with the hermit his name has been always Beau filz. Comp. Libius Disconius, ll. 25—30 and 62—66. Percy folio, vol. ii. p. 416 and 418.

The King
answers, and tells
the story.

' I am þe kynge of þis londe · & oryens am kalled,

And þe 3ondur is my qwene · betryce she hette,   232

¶ In þe 3ondere balowe fyre · is buskedde to brenne ;

She was sklawnndered on-hy3e · þat she hadde takeñ
    howndes ;

And 3yf she hadde so doñ · here harm were not to
    charge.'

' Thou dost ill to
be led by Mata-
bryne.

' Thenne were þou no3t ry3[t]lye sworne,' quod þe
    chylde · ' vpon ry3te Iuge,   236

Whenne þou tokest þe þy crowne · kynge whenne þou
    made were,

To done aftur matabryne · for þenne þou shalt mysfare ,

She is fell and
false, and shall go
to the fiend.

For she is fowle felle & fals · & so she shalle be
    fowndeñ,

And bylefte with þe fend · at here laste ende,   240

¶ That styked styffe in here brestes · þat wolde þe
    qwene brenne :

I am but 12
years old, but I
will fight for the
Queen.'

I am but lytulle & 3onge,' quod þe chylde · ' leeue þou
    forsothe,

Not but twelfe 3ere olde · eueñ at þis tyme,

And I wolle putte my body · to better & to worse, 244

To fy3te for þe qwene · with whome þat wronge
    seythe.'

The King is con-
tent.

Thenne graunted þe kynge · & Ioye he bygynnethe,

If any helpe were þer-Inne · þat here clensen my3te.

The old Queen
rebukes him.

By þat come þe olde qwene · & badde hym com
    þenne :   248

---

233. 3ondere. Misprinted 3onders in
the Roxb. ed.

235. hadde is erroneously printed
shadde in the Roxb. ed.

here harm were not to charge = her
death would not be a matter of concern to any one. ' Charge, in Chaucer,
= a matter of difficulty, a matter of
consideration.'—R. M.

236-7. The French corresponding to
this passage is,

  Arse ! Dieu dist lenfant, fait as
    folle iugement

Nas pas a droit iuge comme roy loy-
  aument.

vpon ry3te Iuge = [hast not] rightly judged.   These words are evidence
that the French poem was the original
of the English one ; our poet having
apparently taken the word Iuge into
his text without translating it.

243. Not but = only.   In modern
Lancashire, no but, or not but.

245. with whom [soever it be] that
wrong saith [of her].

248. þenne = thence.

¶ 'To speke with suche on as he · þou mayste ryȝth
　　lothe thenke.'　　　　　　　　　　　　　249

'A, dame,' quod þe kynge · 'thowȝte ȝe none synne ?

Thow haste for-sette þe ȝonge qwene · þou knoweste
　　welle þe sothe :

This chylde þat I here speke withe · seyth þat he
　　wolle preue　　　　　　　　　　　　　252

That þou nother þy sawes · certeyne be neyther.'

And þenne she lepte to hym · & kawȝte hym by þe
　　lokke ;

That þer lened in here honde · heres an hondredde.

'A, by lyuynge god,' quod þe childe · 'þat bydeste in
　　heuene,　　　　　　　　　　　　　256

¶ Thy hedde shalle lye on þy lappe · for þy false turnes.

I aske a felawe anone · a freshe knyȝte aftur,

For to fyȝte with me · to dryue owte þe ryȝte.'

'A, boy,' quod she, 'wylt þou so · þou shalt sone
　　myskarye ;　　　　　　　　　　　　260

He speaks up for his Queen, and [Fol. 128 b.] tells what the child says.

Matabryne rushes at the child and tears his hair.

'Thy head shall lie in thy lap!' quoth he. 'Give me a man to fight with!'

254. hym, sc. the child. The passage in the French poem is curious, the writer exhibiting the rage of the contending parties by a furious succession of rimes in -aige, the Norman pronunciation of -age.

Mere ce dist le roy vous nestes mie saige
Veez a ung enfant qui bien semble sauvaige
Qui dit que peche faictes et ennuy et hontaige
Que vous la dame a tort vous mettez sur putaige
Quant la vielle lentent a pou quelle nenrage
Aux checeulx prent lenfant plus de c. en arrache
Dieu aide dist lenfant ci a mal a comtaige
Ceste vielle hideuse a en son corps la raige
Plus fait a redoubter que mil lyon sauvaige
La glorieuse dame en qui dieu print umbraige

Menroye en cor rengence de ce villain hontaige ;
Ce ne me faisoit mie mon pere en lermitaige.
Tous ceulx qui lont oy huchent en leur langaige
Ha : roy de orient ne souffrez tel hontaige ;
Li enfant dit assez par les sains de cartaige.
Roy tien a lenfant droit bien pert de hault paraige,
Nulz homs ne puet mieulx dire tant soit de grant langaige,
Dieu te la envoye pour dire cest messaige.

256. bydeste. Sic in MS. 'It is probably thrown in parenthetically, and addressed to God. So in Havelok,
"Ihesu crist, þat made mone,
Þine dremes turne to ioye [sone]
Þat wite þw that sittes in trone."
It is very abrupt, certainly.'—W. W. S. In Havelok also, there is a Thou in the former part of the sentence, but here there is none.

'Ha! boy! I'll get me a man that shall mar thee.'

I wylle gete me a man · þat shalle þe sone marre.'

She turneth her þenne to malkedras · & byddyth hym take armes,

She sends Malkedras.

And badde hym bathe his spere · in þe boyes herte :

And he of suche one · gret skorne he þowȝte.   264

An Abbot christens the child Enyas.

¶ An holy abbot was þer-by · & he hym þeder bowethe,

For to cristen þe chylde · frely & feyre ;

The abbot maketh hym a fonte · & was his godfader,

The erle of aunthepas · he was another,   268

The countes of salamere · was his godmoder ;

They kallede hym Enyas to name · as þe book tellethe :

Mony was þe ryche ȝyfte · þat þey ȝafe hym aftur :

The bells ring of themselves all the fight through, betokening that Christ was well pleased.

Alle þe bellys of þe close · rongen at ones   272

¶ Withe-oute ony mannes helpe · whyle þe fyȝte lasted ;

Wherefore þe wyste welle · þat criste was plesed with here dede.

Whenne he was cristened · frely & feyre,

The King dubs Enyas knight.

Aftur, þe kynge dubbede hym knyȝte · as his kynde wolde :   276

Thenne prestly he prayeth þe kynge · þat he hym lene wolde

The King lends him his good steed Feraunce, and armour, and a shield with a cross on it.

An hors with his harnes · & blethelye he hym grauntethe :

Thenne was feraunce fette forthe · þe kynges price stede,

And out of an hyȝe towre · armour þey halenne ;   280

¶ And a whyte shelde with a crosse · vpon þe posse honged,

And hit was wryten þer-vpon · þat to enyas hit sholde :

261. marre. This is written in the MS. with a long r in the second place; and the former editor mistook it for a y, and wrote the word marye. The word 'miscarrye' in the line above might have undeceived him, for it also has the long r, followed by a real y.

262. þenne. Printed thenee in the Roxb. ed.

263. An holy abbot. ' L'Abbe Gautier,' says the French book.

271. ȝyfte. This is misprinted ȝyste in the 1820 edition.

274. welle. Misprinted welt in the other edition.

279. Feraunce is Ferrant in the French poem.

281. posse. Perhaps miswritten for poste, as Utterson has printed it: it is, however, so written in the MS. Ayenbyte of Inwyt.

282. hit sholde [belong].

And whenne he was armed · to alle his ryȝtes,   283

Thenne prayde he þe kynge · þat he hym lene wolde

Oon of his beste menne · þat he moste truste,

To speke with hym but · a speche whyle.

A knyȝte kawȝte hym by þe honde · & ladde hym of
þe rowte :   287

'What beeste is þis,' quod þe childe · 'þat I shalle on
houe ? '

¶ ' Hit is called an hors,' quod þe knyȝte · ' a good & an
abulle.'

' Why etethe he yren ? ' quod þe chylde · ' wylle he ete
noȝthe elles ?

And what is þat on his bakke · of byrthe, or on
boundeñ ? '

' Nay, þat in his mowthe · men kallen a brydelle,   292

And that a sadelle on his bakke · þat þou shalt in
sytte.'

' And what heuy kyrtelle is þis · withe holes so thykke ?

And þis holowe [on] on my hede · I may noȝt wele
here.'

' An helme men kallen þat on · & an hawberke þat
other.'   296

¶ ' But what broode on is þis on my breste · hit hereth
adowñ my nekke.'

' A bryȝte shelde & a sheene · to shylde þe fro strokes.'

' And what longe on is þis · that I shalle vp lyfte ? '

' Take þat launce vp in þyn honde · & loke þou hym
hytte ;   300

Marginal notes:

Enyas takes counsel with a Knight whom the King lends him,

and learns what is a horse,

a saddle, a bridle, a hawberk, a helm, a shield, a lance, and a [Fol. 129.] sword ; and how to use them.

'See thou hit him.'

---

285. truste, *pf.* of trust; it is *triste* in l. 49.

286. a speche whyle. Comp. Shaksp. Two Gent. of Verona, IV. 3.

287. of = from out of.

288. houe. The Roxb. editor reads *hone*, and takes it to be the O.E. Hon = to hang, but it is doubtless Hove = abide, be.

290. The child puts this question to the King, in the French poem.

291. of byrthe = congenital, born with him, natural.

295. wele. This word is added in the margin in a later hand. It is omitted in the edition of 1820.

holowe = hollow one : the *on* has dropped out, because of the preposition following. See ll. 297, 299.

296. þat other. Misprinted *þe other* in the 1820 edition.

And whenne þat shafte is schyuered · take scharpelye
   another.'

'and if we come
to ground ?'

'Ȝe, what yf grace be · we to grownde wenden ?'

'A-ryse vp lyȝtly on þe fete · & reste þe no lengur ; 303

'Get up again.
Draw thy sword,
smite him with
the edge, snred
him in pieces.'

And þenne plukke out þy swerde · & pele on hym faste,

¶ Alle-wey eggelynges dowñ · on alle þat þou fyndes ;

His ryche helm nor his swerde · rekke þou of neyþur ;

Lete þe sharpe of þy swerde · schreden hym smalle.'

'But won't he
smite again ?'

'But wolle not he smyte aȝeyne · whenne he feleth
   smerte ?'   308

'That will he !
never mind !
smite off his
head ! '

'Ȝys, I knowe hym fulle wele · bothe kenely & faste :

Euur folowe þou on þe flesh · tylle þou haste hym
   fallethe ;

And sythen smyte of his heede · I kan sey þe no
   furre.'

'Now þou haste tawȝte me,' quod þe childe · 'god I þe
   beteche :   312

¶ For now I kan of þe crafte · more þenne I kowthe.'

They run to-
gether, shiver
their spears,

Thenne þey maden Raunges · & roññen to-gedere,

That þe speres in here hondes · shyneredeñ to peces ;

And for [to] renñene aȝeyn · men rawȝten hem other, 316

Of balowe tymbere & bygge · þat wolde not breste ;

And eyther of hem · so smer[t]lye smote other,

smash their
armour, and up-
set each other.

That alle fleye in þe felde · þat on hem was fastened,

And eyther of hem topseyle · tumbledde to þe erthe ; 320

The horses run
round the lists.

¶ Thenne here horses ronnen forth · aftur þe raunges,

Euur ferauñce by-forne · & þat other aftur ;

302. ȝe. Misprinted Se in the edition of 1820.

303. lyȝtly. Misprinted lyȝt in 1820.

305. eggelynges = edgewise. With the edge. The contrary of '*flatlings*.'

307. sharpe = sharp edge.

309. ȝys = yes. Its use here instead of ȝe, as in l. 302, is due to the negative in the question.

310. fallethe = felled.

316. rennene may be *rennenge, sb.;* but more probably the line should be as above, the *to* having been accident-ally omitted by the scribe.

320. topseyle. *Sic* in MS. Top = head,—as we say, 'from *top* to toe.' Should it be perhaps 'topteyle' ? Comp. Wm. of Palerne, l. 2776 :

   'Set hire a sad strok so sore in þe
      necke
   þat sche *top ouer tail* tombled ouer
      þe hacches.'

321. ronnen. Misprinted *rennen* in the Roxb. ed.

322. *Le destrier Elyas va, lautre poursuivant.*

Feraũce launces vp his fete · & lasschethe out his
yeñ :

The fyrste happe, other hele · was þat · þat þe chylde
hadde,   324

Feraũce lashes out and blinds the other horse.

Wheñne þat þe chylde þat hym bare · blente hadde his
fere :

Thenne thei styrte vp on hy · with staloworth shankes,
Pulledde out her swerdes · & smoten to-geduʳ.
'Kepe þy swerde fro my croyse' · quod cheuelrye
assygne :   328

Enyas and Malkedras start up and draw their swords. 'Beware my cross!'

¶ 'I charde not þy croyse,' quod malkedras · 'þe valwe
of a cherye ;

'I don't care a cherry for your cross!'

For I shalle choppe it fulle smalle · ere þenne þis werke
ende.'

An edder spronge out of his shelde · & in his body
spynnethe ;
A fyre fruscheth out of his croys · & [f]rapte out his
yen :   332

An adder strikes him from out the cross; and a fire thereout blinds him.

Thenne he stryketh a stroke · Cheualere assygne,
Eueñ his sholder in twoo · & dowñ in-to þe herte ;
And he bowethe hym dowñ · & ȝeldethe vp þe lyfe.
'I shalle þe ȝelde,' quod þe chylde · 'ryȝte as þe knyȝte
me tawȝte.'   336

Enyas cuts him down and takes [Fol. 129 b.] off his head.

323. yeñ. The transcriber for the
Roxb. ed. mistook the curl over the n
(n) for a d, as if it was rd, and wrote
yerd, making nonsense of the line.
324. hele. The Roxb. ed. has fele ;
which is wrong.
325. chylde. This word seems to
have crept in by mistake. The sense
and alliteration would require 'blonk'
= steed.
326. Thenne thei. The Roxb. ed.
has Thenne ether; the transcriber
having mistaken the last e in then for
the beginning of the word ether.
staloworth. Miswritten for stalworth.
328. cheuelrye. Sic in MS.
330. þenne = the time when.

Un serpent a deux testes,
onques tel ne vit homme
saillit
Qui l'avoit a l'esquarre a sa veue
se lance
Les deux testes lui crevent les deux
yeulx sans doubtance.

332. rapte, in MS.; frapte, which
is a common word enough, would suit
the alliteration better.
333. Thenne. Sic in MS. The Roxb.
ed. has whenne.
334. 'Schreding,' or some such word,
is wanted instead of, or after, Even.
336. I shall þe ȝelde = I shall render
unto thee = I shall serve thee, I shall
requite thee.

¶ He trussethe his harneys fro þe nekke · & þe hede
   wynnethe ;

Sythen he toke hit by þe lokkes · & in þe helm leyde ;

Thoo thanked he our lorde lowely · þat lente hym þat
   grace.

Matabryne flees,
but the child
overtakes her and
has her burnt to
brown ashes.

Thenne sawe þe qwene matabryne · her man so murdered ;   340

Turned her brydelle · & towarde þe towne rydethe ;

The chylde folowethe here aftur · fersly & faste,

Sythen browȝte here aȝeyne · wo for to drye,

And brente here in þe balowe fyer · alle to browne
   askes.   344

The young Queen
is unbound.
Enyas tells his
story to the King
and Queen.

¶ The ȝonge qwene at þe fyre · by þat was vnbounden ;

The childe kome byfore þe kynge · & on-hyȝe he seyde,

And tolde hym how he was his sone · '& oþur sex
   childeren,

By þe qwene betryce · she bare hem at ones,   348

For a worde on þe walle · þat she wronge seyde ;

And ȝonder in a ryuere · swymmen þey swannes ;

Sythen þe forsworne thefe Malkadras · byrafte hem her
   cheynes.'   351

'By god,' quod þe goldsmythe · 'I knowe þat ryȝth wele ;

The goldsmith
says he has five of
the chains at
home.
They all go to
the river and give
the chains to the
swans.
Each choosing
his own, turns to
his human form.
All but one. He,
for want of his
chain, remained
always a swan.

¶ Fyve cheynes I haue · & þey ben fysh hole.'

Nowe withe þe goldsmyȝthe · gon alle þese knyȝtes,

Toke þey þe cheynes · & to þe watur turnen,   355

And shoken vp þe cheynes · þer sterten vp þe swannes ;

Eche on chese to his · & turnen to her kynde :

But on was alwaye a swanne · for losse of his cheyne.

Hit was doole for to se · þe sorowe þat he made ;

He bote hym self with his bylle · þat alle his breste
   bledde,   360

---

345. by þat = by that time.

353. fysh hole = 'as sound as a roach,' as we say.

356. shoken. Sic in MS. The former edition has stroken.

357. turnen. The former edition has turneden in this place ; but not in l. 355.

chese to his = chose his own.

358. alwaye. Sic in MS. Edition of 1820 has always.

¶ And alle his feyre federes · fomede vpon blode,

And alle formerknes þe watur · þer þe swanne swym-
    methe :

There was ryche ne pore · þat myȝte for rewthe,   'Twas sad to see
                                                       his sorrow.
Lengere loke on hym · but to þe courte wendeñ.   364

Thenne þey formed a fonte · & cristene þe childreñ ;   They christen the
                                                        children.
And callen Vryens þat on · and Oryens another,

Assakarye þe thrydde · & gadyfere þe fowrthe ;

The fyfte hette rose · for she was a maydeñ ;   368

The sixte was fulwedde · chenelere assygne.

And þus þe botenynge of god · browȝte hem to honde.;.   So by God's help
                                                        they were
                                                        restored.

.;. EXPLICIT .;.

---

362. formerknes. If this is v.
intr., and governed by the sb. water,
it should have been by rights former-
keneth ; but if it is pl. and tr. governed
by federes, it has borrowed the Northern -es termination instead of the Midland -en.

366. The names of the children in
the French poem are Orions, Orient,
Zacharias, Jehan, and Rosette.

369. was fulwedde = had been baptized already.

GLOSSARIAL INDEX.

ABBREVIATIONS.

Adj.	= Adjective.	*Obj.*	= Objective.
Adv.	= Adverb.	*O.E.*	= Old English, A. D. 500
Allit.	= Early Engl. Alliterative		—1200.
	Poems.	*Pf.*	= Perfect.
Art.	= Article.	*Pl.*	= Plural.
Comp.	= Comparative.	*P. pt.*	= Past Participle.
Conj.	= Conjunction.	*Pers.*	= Personal.
Cp.	= Compare.	*Poss.*	= Possessive.
Dem.	= Demonstrative.	*Prep.*	= Preposition.
Fem.	= Feminine.	*Pron.*	= Pronoun.
Fr.	= French.	*Refl.*	= Reflexive.
Gen.	= Genesis and Exodus.	*Rel.*	= Relative.
Germ.	= German.	*Sb.*	= Substantive.
Imp.	= Imperative.	*Sc.*	= Scottish.
Imp. pt.	= Imperfect Participle.	*Sing.*	= Singular.
Int.	= Interjection.	*Tr.*	= Transitive.
Intr.	= Intransitive.	*V.*	= Verb.

Wm. = William of Palerne.

A, *interj.* = Ah, 71, 82, 250, 255, 260.

A, *art.* 5, 6, &c. Perhaps as a numeral = one, 157, 165.

A, *prep.* = in, or on ; O.E. & O. Sc. *An.* In l. 79 it means *at.*

Abbot, *sb.* 265.

Abowte, *prep.* 44, 126.

Abulle, *adj.* = fit, proper, able, 289.

Adowne, *adv.* = down, 21, 88, 101, 114; adown, 190, 297.

Affye, *sb.* = trust, 10.

Afore, *adv.* = in front, 228.

Aftur, *prep.* = along, 321 ; for, or in quest of, 46, 129, 153, 342 ; in accordance with, 13, 238 ; *adv.* = afterwards, 54, 80, 258, 271, 276 ; behind, 322.

Alle, *adj.* 43, 67, 98, &c.; *adv.* 15.

Alle-weldinge, *adj.* = Almighty, 1. O.E. *Eal-wealdende.*

Allewey. *See* Alwaye.

Allone, *adj.* = alone, 184.

Als, *conj.* = also, 91.

Also, *conj.* 218.

Alwaye, *adv.* 358 ; allewey, 305.

An, *art.* 5, 331, &c.

And, *conj.* 8, 18, &c. = an, if, 139.

Angelle, *sb.* 192, 193, 221.

Anon, *adv.* 85 ; anone, 68, 190, 258.

Another, *adj.* 268, 301, 366.

Ar, 3*d pl. pres. ind.* of *v.* Be, 82.

Armed, *p. pt.* of arm, *v. tr.* 283.

Armes, *sb. pl.* 262.

Armour, *sb.* 280.

Aryse, *v. intr.* 2*d sing. imper.* 77, 303.

As, *conj.* 7, 19, &c. = as though, 53.

Aske, *v. tr.* 128, 171 ; 3*d sing. pf.* askede, 130, 192 ; asskede, 210; *p. pt.* asked, 131.

Askes, *sb. pl.* = ashes, 344.

Asseylde, 3*d sing. pf. ind.* of asseyle, *v. tr.* 145.

Assygne = Fr. an cygne, 11, &c.

Assygyned, *p. pt.* of assign, *v. tr.* 188.

At, *prep.* 23, 60, 98.

Awȝte, *sb.* = aught, 204.

Aȝeyne, *adv.* = again, 93, 104, 137, 177, 343 ; aȝeyn, 123.

Badde. *See* Bid.

Bakke, *sb.* = back, 291, 293.

Balowe, *adj.* O.E. *Bealu*, or *Bealo; Balo* or *Balu* = deadly, 233, 344, strong (?) 317.

Banke, *sb.* 132.

Barmeteme, *sb.* 103. This is the O.E. *Bearnteme*, and is miswritten for barnteme = brood, progeny, from barne = child, bairn ; and teme, or teem (O.E. *teman*) = to produce, bring forth. *See* Gen. 954 and 3903. In Chalmers's Life of James I. (prefixed to his 'Poetic Remains of the Scottish kings,' 1824), p. 15, he writes, "The Act of the former session was renewed in this ; requiring the clergy to pray for the king, for the queen, and their *Bairntime*, which is now explained to mean, 'the children produced between them.'"

Bathe, *v. tr.* 263.

Bare, 3*d sing. pf. ind.* of bear, *v. tr.* 325, 348.

Be, *v. intr.* 17, 37, 80 ; 3*d pl. pres. subj.* bene (O.E. *beon*), 188; 3*d sing. subj.* 100, 302.

Bedde, *sb.* 33, 161.

Beetheth. *See* Bete.

Befalle, *v. intr.* 204.

Bene. *See* Be, *v. intr.*

Bere, *v. tr.* 3*d sing. ind.* bereth, 207; 3*d sing. pf.* 196. *See also* Bare, *p. pt.* borne, 23, 41.

Berthe. *See* Byrthe.

Beste, *sb.* = beast, 214 ; beeste, 218, 288.

Beste, *adj.* 68, 285.

Bete, *v. tr.* O.E. *betan* = to prepare, to kindle (said of fire); 3*d sing. pres. ind.* beetheth, 157 ; *p. pt.* bette, 224.

Bete, *v. tr.* = beat ; *imp. pt.* betynge, 227.

Beteche, *v. tr. See* Bytake, 312.

Bette. *See* Bete.

Better, *adj.* 49, 175 ; bettur, *adv.* 97.

Betyde, *v. intr.* 103.

Betynge. *See* Bete.

Bid, *v. tr.* 3*d sing. pf.* badde, 156, 172, 248, 263 ; 3*d sing. pres.* byddyth, 262.

Bledde, 3*d sing. pf.* of bleed, *v. intr.* 360.

Blente, *p. pt.* of blind, *v. tr.*
O.E. *blendian*, 325.

Blethely, *adv.* = blithely, cheer-
fully, 278.

Blode, *sb.* = blood, 361.

Blythe, *adj.* 154.

Body, *sb.* 244.

Book, *sb.* 7, 270.

Borne. *See* Bere, *v. tr.*

Bote, 3*d sing. pf.* of bite, *v. tr.*
360.

Botenning, *sb.* = remedy, succour,
370; from boten, *v. tr.* formed from
bote = remedy, from O.E. *gebetan*
= to mend.

Bothe, *conj.* 20, 79; *adj.* 135.

Bounden, *p. pt.* of bind, *v. tr.*
291.

Boy, *sb.* 260; *poss.* boyes, 263.

Bowethe, 3*d sing. pres. ind.* of
bow, *v. tr.* 335; bowethe hym,
265 = turneth him, goeth.

Breke, *v. tr.* O.E. *brecan;* 3*d
sing. pres.* brekethe, 157; 1*st sing.
pf. ind.* breke (now brake, or broke),
165.

Brenne, *v. tr.* = burn, 68, 241;
pf. brente, 344; *p. pt.* brente, 80;
intransitively, 191, 224.

Breste, *sb.* 297, 360; *pl.* brestes,
241.

Breste, *v. inter.* = burst, 317.

Broode, *adj.* = broad, 297.

Browne, *adj.* 344.

Browȝte, 3*d sing. pf.* of bring, *v.
tr.* 41, 49, 343, 370.

Brydelle, *sb.* 229, 292, 341.

Brynge, *v. tr.* 2*d sing. imp.* 203.

Bryȝt, *adj.* = bright, 8; bryȝte,
298.

Busk, *v. tr.* = prepare, make
ready; 3*d sing. pf. ind.* buskede,
172; *p. pt.* buskedde, 233.

But, *conj.* 15, 17, &c. = except,
38; only, 242.

By, *prep.* 196, 348; = of, concerning, 5; at, about, 84, 143,
205; through, 85, 216, *adv.* =
near, 109.

Bycche, *sb.* = bitch, 62.

Bydeste = abidest, 256, 2*d sing.
ind.* of byde, *v. intr.*

Byddynge, *sb.* = command, 85.

Byddyth. *See* Bid.

Byfore, *prep.* = before, 23, 64,
110, 124, &c., before, 114.

Byforne, *adv.* = before, 322 (Wm.
biforn. Gen. *biforen*).

Bygyleth, *p. pt.* of beguile, *v. tr.*
(for beguiled), 78.

Byginne, *v. tr.* 3*d sing. pres. ina.*
bygynnethe, 76, 246; 3*d sing. pf.*
byganne, 183.

Byhelde, 3*d sing. pf.* of byhold =
behold, 21.

Bylefte, *p. pt.* of byleve, or be-
leave = abandon, 240.

Bylle, *sb.* = bill, 360.

Byrafte, 3*d sing. pf. ind.* of by-
reave *or* bereave. O.E. *bereafian;*
199, 351.

Byrthe, *sb.* = birth, 23, 40, 291;
berthe, 65.

Byside, *adv.* = beside, 149.

Bytake (*or* bitake) = betake, com-
mit, deliver. O.E. *betæcan;* 3*d
sing. pres. ind.* bytakethe, 151;
bytaketh, 173; *p. pt.* bytaken, 163;
cp. Gen. 212.

Call, *v. tr.* 3*d pl. pres. indic.*
callen, 366; kallen, 292, 206; 3*d
pl. pf.* called, 46; kallede, 270; 2*d
sing. imp.* kalle, 204; *p. pt.* called,
289; kalled, 6, 231.

Caste, *v. tr.* 52; 3*d pl. pres. ind.*
caste, 88; 1*st sing. pf.* caste, 167;
3*d sing.* caste, 63.

Cawsed, 3*d sing. pf. ind.* of
cause, *v. tr.* 39

Certeyne, *adj.* = certain, 253.

Charde, *v. intr.* = care, 329.

Charge, *sb.* concern, 235.

Chaste, *sb.* = chest, 127. *See* Note.

Chaunce, *sb.* 123.

Chefe, *sb.* = chief, 11.

Cherye, *sb.* = cherry, 329.

Chese, 3*d sing. pf.* of choose. Used with the *prep.* to, 357.

Cheualere, *sb.* 11, 333; cheuelere, 369.

Cheuelrye, *sb.* miswritten for cheuelere, 328.

Cheuene, *v. tr.* quasi chiefen = to rule over, 16.

Cheuerynge, *imp. pt.* of cheuer *or* chyuer, q. v.

Cheyne, *sb.* 43, 125, 137, 146, 148, 150, 157, 164, 165, 176, 179, 199, 351.

Choppe, *v. tr.* 330.

Chylde, *sb.* = child, 16, 29, &c. With chylde, 35; *pl.* chylderen, 23, 82, 93; chyldren, 107, 122, 130, &c.; children, 143; childeren, 347.

Chyuer, *v. intr.* = shiver, 3*d pl. pf.* chyuered, 107; *imp. pt.* cheuerynge, 107. Cp. Morte Arthur (Linc.) l. 3392.

Clene, *adj.* 174.

Clensen, *v. tr.* = to cleanse, 247.

Close, *sb.* = an enclosed field, or space of ground, 272.

Clothe, *sb.* = cloth, 97.

Colde, *sb.* 107.

Combred (*p. pt.* of combre (cumber) = to trouble) = miserable, 71.

Come, *v. intr.* 38; com, 248; 2*d sing. pres. indic.* comeste, 51; 3*d sing.* comethe, 109; *pf.* come, 64, 110, 142, 151, 173, 183, 208, 228, 248; Kome, 113, 346; *p. pt.* comen, 154.

Confounde, *v. tr.* 75.

Countes, *sb.* = countess, 269.

Counselle, *sb.* 50.

Courte, *sb.* 53, 123, 163, 203; cowrte, 150, 155, &c.

Cowche, *sb.* = bed, 45.

Cowpe, *sb.* = cup, 153, 164, 173, &c.

Crafte, *sb.* = business, 313.

Criste, 104; Cryste, 111.

Cristen, *v. tr.* = christen, 266; 3*d pl. pres. ind.* cristene, 365; *p. pt.* cristened, 203, 275.

Crosse, *sb.* 281.

Crowne, *sb.* 237.

Croyse, *sb.* = cross, 328-9; croys, 332.

Cry, *v. intr.* 3*d sing. pres. ind.* cryethe, 81; 3*d pl. pf.* cryedde, 106; cryde, 108; cryede, 111.

Cuppe, *sb.* 160, 168.

Cursed, *p. pt.* of curse, *v. tr.* 38, 145; used adjectively, cursede, 142; cursedde, 121.

Curteynesse, *sb.* = courteousness, 179.

Dame, *sb.* 69, 73, 125, 132, 250.

Damme, *sb.* = mother, 61.

Dare, *v. intr.* 1*st sing. pres. ind.* 27; 3*d sing. pf.* durste, 56; *pl.* 147.

Day, *sb.* 188, 191, 208.

Dedde. *See* Done.

Dede, *sb.* = deed, 274.

Deepe, *adv.* 86.

Delyuered, *p. pt.* of delyuer, *v. tr.* 37, 180; 3*d sing. pf.* 155, 178.

Deseruethe, 3*d sing. pres.* of deserve, *v. tr.* 72.

Deth, *sb.* 100; dethe, 138, 182, 186.

Do, *v. tr.* 139; done, 238; 3*d sing. pf.* 172; 2*d sing. imper.* do, 138 *p. pt.* don, 235.

Dole, *sb.* = sorrow, compassion, 134; doole, 359.

Dolefulle, *adj.* 106.

Dome, *sb.* = doom, 186 ; *pl.* domus, 91.

Dore, *sb.* 60, 87.

Down, *adv.* 305, 334, 335.

Dowȝter, *sb.* = daughter, 42.

Draw, *v. tr.* O.E. *dragan* (intransitively used, as in the phrase 'Draw near'); 3*d sing.* and *pl.* drowȝ, 33 ; and drowȝe, 37, 114, 161.

Drowȝe = drew (Gen. 1. 2360, dragen. O.E. *drog*). *See* Draw.

Drye, *v. tr.* (O.E. *dreogan.* Gen. *dregen;* Allit. *dryȝe*) = to dree, to suffer, 343.

Dryue, *v. tr.* dryue out = bring out, ascertain, 259.

Dubbode, 3*d sing. pf. ind.* 276.

Durste. *See* Dare.

Dwellest, 2*d sing. pres. ind.* of dwell, *v. intr.* 201; 3*d sing. pf.* dwellede, 13.

Dymme, *adj.* = dim, dark, 86.

Dynte, *sb.* 138.

Eche, *adj.* = each, 31, 44, 126 ; each a, O.E. *ilka* = each, every, 187.

Edder, *sb.* = adder, 331.

Eggelynges, *adv.* = edgelings, edgewise, with the edge (O.E. *Ecg.* = edge), 305.

Eke, *adv.* = also, 180.

Elles, *adv.* = else (Allit. *elleȝ*), 74, 215, 290; ellis, 30.

Elleven, *adj.* 89.

Ende, *sb.* 40, 240 ; *v. tr.* 330.

Enforme, *v. tr.* 212.

Er, *prep.* = ere, before, 70.

Erle, *sb.* 268.

Erthe, *sb.* 320.

Etethe, 3*d sing. pres. ind.* of ete (eat), 290.

Euen, 243, 334.

Euur = ever, 222, 322.

Eyther = each, 220, 318, 320.

Fader, *sb.* = father, 90, 212, 219 ; *poss.* fader, 203.

Fallethe, *p. pt.* of fall = falled, 310. Perhaps miswritten for *felled;* which is the more likely, as the *p. pt.* of *fall* ought to be *fallen;* while *fell* would make *felled.* We say, however, sometimes, 'To *fall* timber.'

False, *adj.* 257 ; fals, 239.

Faste, *adv.* 141, 223, 227, 304, 309, 342.

Fastened, *p. pt.* of fasten, *v. tr.* 319.

Fayre, *adj.* 90 ; feyre, 217, 266, 275, 361.

Febull, *adj.* = sad, bad, 58 ; used *substantively,* 76.

Feder, *sb.* = feather; *pl.* federes, 361.

Felawe, *sb.* = fellow, 258.

Felde, *sb.* = field, 223, 319.

Felle, *adj.* = severe, stern, cruel, 239.

Felle, *pf.* of fall, *v. intr.* 110, 114; 3*d pl.* 148 ; = befell, 130.

Felly, *adv.* = sternly, cruelly, fiercely, 76, 225. The word is used by Spenser.

Fende, *sb.* = fiend, devil, 120 ; fend, 240.

Fere, *sb.* = companion, 325.

Fersly, *adv.* = fiercely, 342.

Ferther, *adv.* (*comp.*) = further, 127.

Fete, *sb.* (*pl.* of foot) 303, 323.

Fette, *p. pt.* of fette, *v. tr.* = fetch, 279.

Graunt, *v. tr.* = grant ; 2*d sing. pf. ind.* grauntethe, 278; 3*d sing.* graunted, 189, 246.

Grete, *adj.* = great, 83 ; gret, 264.

Grownde, *sb.* 302.

Grymme, *adj.* black, dark, 51 ; sad, 189. Cp. Allit. A. 1069.

Grypte, 3*d sing. pf.* of gryp, *v. tr.* 220.

Gynnyth, 3*d sing. pres. ind.* of gynne, *v.* (begin), 66.

Hadde. *See* Haue.

Halen, *v. tr.* = to haul ; 3*d pl. indic.* halenne, 280.

Halfe, *sb.* 165 ; = side, behalf, 219.

Halueñdele = half-deal = half, 176 ; halvendelle, 160.

Ham, *pers. pron. obj.* = them, 152.

Happe, *sb.* = hap (good), 324.

Harm, *sb.* 235 ; harme, 3.

Harnes, *sb.* = armour, 278 ; harneys, 337.

Hast. *See* Haue.

Hatefulle, *adj.* 141.

Hath. *See* Haue.

Haue, *v. tr.* 120 ; 1*st sing. pres. ind.* 70, 353; 2*d sing.* hast, 78 ; haste, 194, 251, 310; 3*d sing.* hath, 128; 3*d pl.* haue, 79; 3*d sing. pf.* hadde, 16, 44, 47 ; 1*st sing. pf. subj.* 181; 2*d sing.* 53; *p. pt.* hadde, 79.

Hawberke, *sb.* 296.

He, *pers. pron.* 2, 13, &c.

Hedde, *sb.* = head, 27, 217, 257 ; hede, 295 ; heede, 311.

Heelde. *See* Holden, *v. tr.*

Heete (or Hete), *v. tr.* = tell ; 1*st sing. pres. indic.* 18.

Hele, *sb.* = pleasure, advantage, 324. O.E. *Hel* = health.

Helle, *sb.* 10.

Helme = helmet, *sb.* 296, 306, 338.

Helpe, *sb.* 118, 247, 273.

Helpe, *v. tr.* 50 ; 3*d sing. pres. subj.* 70.

Hem, *pron.* = 'em, them ; 19, 20, 44, 45, 52, 83, 96, 97, 101, 102, 104, 109, 110, 112, 114—119, 126, 129, 133, 134, 138, 148, 151, 152, 159, 169, 190, 194, 196, 199, 316, 318—320, 348, 351.

Hemselfen = themselves, 20.

Hente, *v. tr.* = seize, take ; 3*d pl. pf. ind.* hente, 85 ; *p. pt.* hente, 3.

Her, *poss. pron. fem.* 10, 32, 340, 341.

Her, *pers. pron. fem. obj.* 23, 35, 38, 47, 68, 70, 73, 85, 176, 262.

Her, *adv.* = here, in this place, 77.

Her = their. *See* Here.

Here, *poss. pron. fem.* = her, 171, 182, 240, 255.

Here, *pers. pron. fem. obj.* = her, 15, 32, 34, 86—88, 126, 131, 135, 151, 153, 189, 190, 226, 342—344.

Here, *poss. pron. pl.* = their, 126, 220, 235, 274, 315, 321 ; her, 105, 199, 327.

Here, *v. tr.* = hear, 57 ; 1*st sing. pf. ind.* herde, 213 ; 3*d sing.* 55, 58, 108 ; 2*d sing. imper.* 131.

Here, *sb.* = hair ; *pl.* heres, 255.

Heremyte, *sb.* 115, 221 ; hermyte, 109, 192, 201.

Herseluen = herself, 47.

Herte, *sb.* (Germ. *herz*) = heart, 18, 189, 263, 334.

Hette, 3*d sing. pres. indic.* = is called, 232 ; 3*d sing. pf.* hette, 7 ; hyȝte, 9. (O.E. *hatan* = to be called.)

His, *poss. pron. masc.* 2, 8, 36, &c.; hys, 135.

Hit, *pers. pron. neut.* 30, 72, 74, &c.

Holden, *v. tr.* = to hold, 169; *3d sing. pf. ind.* heelde, 152; *2d sing. imper.* holde, 127; *p. pt.* holde = accounted, 70.

Hole, *sb.* 294.

Hole, *adj.* = whole, 353.

Hollye, *adv.* = wholly, 160, 168, 181.

Holy, *adj.* 109, 265.

Honde, *sb.* = hand, 2, 41, 152, 158, 164, 166, 174, 220, 255, 287, 300, 315, 370.

Hondredde = hundred, 255.

Honged, *3d sing. pf.* of hongen, or hangen = hang, 18.

Hors, *sb.* = horse, 213, 289; *pl.* horses, 321.

Houe, *v. intr.* = to abide still, to hover, to wait, 288. Cp. Allit. B. 927; and Lancelot, 996.

How, *adv.* 26, 31, &c.

Hownde, *sb. pl.* howndes, 79, 234.

Hy, *adj.* = high, 326; hye, 217; hyȝ, 224; byȝe, 280; on hyȝe = aloud.

Hylyde, *3d sing. pf.* of hylen = hele = cover, 102.

Hym, *pers. pron. masc. obj.* = him, 4, 24, &c.

Hym *for* Hem = them, 52.

Hynde, *sb.* 113, 116.

Hytte, *v. tr.* 300.

Hyȝe, *adj. See* Hy.

Hyȝe, *v. intr.* = hie, go, 139; *refl. 3d sing. pf.* hyed hym, 141.

Hyȝnes, *sb.* = highness, 4.

Hyȝte = was called. *See* Hette.

I, *pers. pron.* 5, 18, &c.

If, *conj.* 192.

In, *prep.* 4, 5, &c.

Is, *3d sing. pres. ind.* of Be, *v. intr.* 1, 26, &c.

It, *pers. pron. neut.* 1, 12, &c.

Joye, *sb.* 246.

Juge = judge, 236. *See* Note.

Kalled, &c. *See* Call.

Kan, *v. tr.* = can, i. e. know; *1st sing. pres. ind.* kan, 311, 313; *2d sing.* kanste, 212; *1st sing. pf.* kowthe = knew, 313.

Kawȝte, *3d sing. pf. ind.* of catch, 287; in l. 62 it = snatched. Cp. 'caught up.'

Keene, *adj.* 183; used *adverbially.*

Kenely, *adv.* 309.

Kepe, *v. tr.* = keep, 50; *3d sing. pf. ind.* kepte, 117, 174; *2d sing. imper.* kepe, 328.

Keste, *3d sing. pf. indic.* of cast, 97.

Knee, *sb. pl.* knees, 110.

Knowe, *v. tr.* 97; *1st sing. pres. ind.* 309, 352; *2d sing.* knoweste, 251; *3d sing. pf.* knewe, 49.

Knyfe, *sb.* 62.

Knyȝte, *sb.* = knight, 258, 276, 287, 289; *pl.* knyȝtes, 354.

Kome. *See* Come.

Kowarde, *sb.* 71.

Kowth. *See* Kan.

Kylled, *3d sing. pf.* of kylle (kill); *v. tr.* 62.

Kynde, *sb.* (kind) = nature, condition, 71, 276; kin, family. 11. Cp. Gen. 650.

Kynge, *sb.* 7, 20, &c.; *poss.* kynges, 195.

Kyrtelle, *sb.* 294.

Ladde. *See* Lead, *v. tr.* Spenser uses this inflection, F. Q., I. i. 4: 'a milke white lamb she *lad.*'

Lady, *sb.* 82, 89, 92, 191.

Lafte. *See* Leve, *v. tr.*

Langour, *sb.* = languor, 15, 57, 92.

Lappe, *sb.* 257.

Lappe, *v. tr.* = wrap ; *3d sing. pf.* lappede, 102 ; *p. pt.* lapped, 132 ; lappedde, 101.

Lassche, *v. tr.* = strike (lash out = kick) ; *3d sing pres. ind.* lasscheth, 323.

Laste, *adj.* 240.

Launce, *sb.* 300.

Launce, *v. tr.* = launce, dart, throw ; *3d sing. pres. ind.* launces, 323.

Laye. See Lye, *v. intr.*

Lead, *v. tr. 3d sing. pf. ind.* ladde, 287.

Lefe, *adj.* = dear, 82.

Lefte, *pf.* of leve, q. v.

Lefte, *3d sing. pf. ind.* of lift (O.E. *Lefan*), 45.

Lende, *v. intr.* a form of leng = tarry, abide ; *p. pt.* lente, ' was lente,' l. 5 = dwelt. Cp. Allit. B. 1084, ' wazt lent.'

Lendeth, *3d sing. pres. ind.* of lend, *v. tr.* 99.

Lene, *v. tr.* = lend, grant, 277, 284 ; *p. pt.* lente, 112, 339.

Leng, *v. intr.* = tarry, dwell ; *3d sing. pres. ind.* lengeth, 4.

Lengur, *adv., comp.* of long, 77, 112, 303 ; lengere, 364.

Lente. See Lende, *v. intr.;* and Lene, *v. tr.*

Lepte, *3d sing. pf. ind.* of lepe (leap), *v. intr.* 254.

Let, *v. tr.* = allow, cause ; *3d sing. pf. ind.* lette, 24, 190; *2d sing. imper.* lette, 187 ; lete, 307 ; *2d sing. subj.* lete, 52.

Leue, *v. tr.* = believe, allow, 28, 133 ; lecue, 242.

Leue, *v. tr.* = leave ; *1st sing. pf. ind.* lafte, 133 ; *3d sing.* 17, 221 ; *1st pl. imper.* leue, 92 ; *3d pl. pres. ind.* leuen, 87. Also *intransitively* = remain ; *3d sing. pf. ind.* lefte, 175 ; leued, 255.

Leues, *sb. pl.* of lefe (leaf), 119.

Ley. See Lye, *v. intr.*

Leyde, *1st sing. pf. ind.* of lay ; *v. tr.* 165 ; *3d sing.* 87, 101, 159, 338.

Leyne, *v. tr.* = grant, requite, reward, 99.

Lofe, *sb.* = love, 15.

Loke, *v. intr.* = look, 364 ; *3d sing. pf. ind.* loked, 21 ; *3d sing. imper.* looke, 52 ; loke, 203, 300.

Lokke, *sb.* of a door, 87 ; of hair, 254 ; *pl.* lokkes, 338.

Londe, *sb.* = land, 6, 181, 231 ; *pl.* londis, 16.

Longe, *adj.* 95, 299 ; *adv.* 47, 185.

Lorde, *sb.* 5, 36, 70, &c.

Lordeles, *adj.* = having no lord, or sovereign, 17.

Losse, *sb.* 358.

Lothe, *adj.* 249 ; loth, 48.

Loue, *sb.* 36.

Loue, *v. tr.* 14.

Louely, *adv.* 98.

Lowde, *adj.* 225.

Lowely, *adv.* = meekly, humbly, 36, 339.

Lowze, *3d pl. pf. indic.* of laze, *v. intr.* = laugh, 98.

Lye, *v. intr.* 257 ; *3d sing. pf. ind.* lay, 57, 207 ; laze, 76 ; *3d pl.* ley, 98 ; *imp. pt.* lyyinge, 133.

Lyf, *sb.* = life, 17 ; lyfe, 112, 335.

Lyfe, *v. intr.* = live, 54.

Lyfte, *v. tr.* 299.

Lyke, *v.* = like, 54 (*see* Note), 140 ; *3d sing. pres. ind.* lykes, 134; lyketh, 73.

Lykynge, *sb.* = liking, 13.

Lyme, *sb.* = limb ; *pl.* lymes, 217.

Lyonys, *pl.* of lyon ; *sb.* 214.

Lytulle, *adj.* 242.

Lyne, *v. intr.* = live; *3d sing. pf. ind.* lyuede, 89.

Lyne, *sb.* = life, 140.

Lyninge, *adj.* = living, 256.

Lyȝtly, *adv.* = lightly, 303.

Made. } See Make.
Maden. }

Make, *v. tr. 3d sing. pres. ind.* maketh, 267; *3d sing. pf.* made, 9, 83, 90, 135, 359; *3d pl.* maden, 314.

Man, *sb.* 46, 108, &c.; manne, 29; *poss.* mannes, 273; *pl.* men, 79, 94; menne, 285.

Mantelle, *sb.* 101, 105, 132.

Many, *adj.* 31, 34, &c.

Marre, *sb.* = mar, *v. tr.* 261.

Mater, *sb.* = matter, 216.

May, *1st sing. pres. ind.* of mowe = to be able = can, 74, 295; *2d sing.* 50, 54; also mayste, 249.

Mayden, *sb.* 368.

Me, *indeterm. pron.* (Germ. *man;* Fr. *on*) 30.

Me, *pers. pron. obj.* 70, 261.

Mene, *v. tr.* mention; *3d sing. pf. ind.* menede, 124.

Mengynge, *sb.* = mingling, twisting, 125. From menge, *v. tr.* = mix.

Meruelows, *adj.* (used *adverbially*) 185.

Meruecyle, *sb.* 125.

Mesure, *sb.* 171.

Mete, *sb.* = meat, 88, 144.

Moche, *adj.* = much, 9, 39, 102, 136; *substantively,* 184.

Moder, *sb.* = mother, 9, 39, 59, 180, 200, 205, 209, 210.

Mone, *sb.* = moan, 83, 136.

Mony, *adj.* 90, 124, 271.

More, *adj.* 88, 125, 171.

Morn, *sb.* = morning, 183.

Morne, *v. intr.* = mourn, 66.

Morwe, *sb.* = morrow, 172.

Most, *v.* = must, *2d sing. ind.* of mot, 50, 206; *3d sing.* 136, 206. *See* Mote.

Moste, *adv.* 285.

Mote, *3d sing. pres. subj.* of mot, 120. The word has in this phrase an optative force. *See* Most.

Mowthe, *sb.* = mouth, 292.

Multiplyeth, *3d sing. pres. ind.* of multiply; *v. intr.* 158.

Murdered, *p. pt.* of murder, *v. tr.* 340.

Murther, *v. tr.* 94, 129.

My, *poss. pron.* 27, 78, 82, 100, &c

Mydday, *sb.* 205.

Myle, *sb.* 95.

Myne, *poss. pron.* 181.

Mysfare, *v. intr.* = go wrong, 238.

Myskarye, *v. intr.* = miscarry, 260.

Myssede, *3d sing. pf. ind.* of mysse (miss), *v. tr.* 83.

Myȝte = might, *1st sing. pf. ind.* of mowe, or mowen, *v.* 134; *3d sing.* 14, 247, 363; *1st pl.* 3.

Name, *sb.* 204, 270.

Nay, *interj.* 28.

Ne = not, 3, 147.

Nekke, *sb.* 297, 337.

Nere, *prep.* = near, 38.

Nere, *v.* = ne were, 4.

Neuur, *adv.* = never, 202, 216.

Neythur, *adv.* 253; *sb.* 306.

No, *adj.* 16, 38, 77.

None = ne one, 127, 216: *adj.* 250.

Noryscheth, *3d sing. pres. ind.* of norysch (nourish); *v. tr.* 118.

Not, *adv.* 28.

Nother, *conj.* = nor, 253.

Nowe, *adv.* 354.

Nowʒte, *sb.* = nought, 53.

Noyse, *sb.* 225.

Noʒt, *adv.* = not, 236, 295; noʒte, 74.

Noʒthe, *sb.* = nought, 290; nowʒte, 53.

Nykke, *v. tr.* = refuse, contradict; = ne (not), ikke (say); cognate with Latin *Negare.* With *ikke* compare Gothic *Aikan;* Sanskrit *Ah* = to say, to speak; Latin *Ajo* (agjo). Cp. also the Sanskrit *Aham* = I, with the O.E. *Ic.*

Nyʒe, *adj.* = nigh, 100.

Nyʒte, *sb.* = night, 33, 34, 161, 191.

Of, *prep.* 4, 10, &c. = from, out of, 287; = *adv.* off, 146, 311.

Ofte, *adv.* 3, 111.

Olde, *adj.* 163, 227, 243, &c.

On, *prep.* 34, 207.

On, *num.* = one, 44, 126, 143, 249, 295, 297, 299, 357, 358; oon, 29, 285.

One, *num.* 264.

One, *adj.* = alone, 15, 19.

Ones, *adv.* = at ones = at once, 98, 196, 272, 348.

On-hyʒe, *adv.* = aloud, 25, 64, 106, 234, 346; on hyʒ, 81; on-hy = up, 326.

Ony, *adj.* = any, 175, 273.

Oo-lyuynge, *adj.* = everliving, eternal, 201.

Oon. *See* On.

Orysoun, *sb.* = prayer, 90.

Other, *adj.* 144, 145, 296, &c.; othur, 159, 167, 347.

Other, *conj.* = or (Germ. *oder*), 324.

Our, *poss. pron.* 36, 70, 93, 117.

Out, *for* drew, *or* pulled out, 146.

Ouur, *adv.* = over, 175.

Owne, 2, 14, &c.

Pappe, *sb.* = breast, 114.

Paye, *v. tr.* = please, 65.

Peces, *pl.* of pece (piece), 315.

Pele, *v. intr.* smite, 'let drive,' 304. Cp. peal (of bells), *sb.*; also pelt, *v.* Mr Skeat writes, "Perhaps this is an instance of the word *Pelle*, which occurs in Havelok, and *nowhere else*, unless it is *here.* In Havelok it = drive forth, go; and seems to be the Lat. *pellere.*

The line in Havelok is,

'Shal ich neuere lenger dwelle,
To morwen shall ich forth *pelle.*'
ll. 809-10.

['I shall stay here no longer,
I shall start off to-morrow!

It answers to our expression, 'go *full drive.*'"

Place, *sb.* 12.

Plesed, *p. pt.* of plese (please); *v. tr.* 274.

Plukke, *v. tr.* 2d *sing. imper.* 304.

Pore, *adj.* = poor, 22, 26, 363.

Posse, *sb.* Perhaps miswritten for Poste, 281.

Prayde, *3d sing. pf. ind.* of pray; *v. tr.* 284; 2d *sing. pres.* prayeth, 277.

Preste, *adj.* = ready, 135.

Prestly, *adv.* = readily, quickly, 277.

Preve, *v. tr.* = prove, 252.

Price, *adj.* = worthy, noble, 279. Comp. Wm. l. 411.

Prisoun, *sb.* 80; prysoun, 86.

Prowde, *adj.* 115.

Pulledde, 3*d pl. pf.* of pulle; *v. tr.* 327.

Putte, *v. tr.*, 3*d sing. pf. ind.* putte, 115; putt, 135.

Pyne, *sb.* = suffering, 92. O.E. *pin*; *v. tr.* = to make to suffer, to torment, 26. O.E. *pinan.*

Pytte, *sb.* = pit, 63.

Quod *or* quoth, 3*d sing. pf. ind.* = said, 71, 99, 169, 214—216, 219, 230, 236, 242, 250, 256, 260, 288, 289, 290, 312, 323-29, 336, 352. O.E. *cwæð*, of *Cweðan* = to say.

Qwene, *sb.* = queen, 8, 14, &c.

Raunges, *sb. pl.* = lists, 314, 321. Cp. 'ringes' in Sir Eglamore, l. 1121, Percy folio, p. 382, vol. 2.

Rawʒte (Raught). *See* Reche.

Reasonabullye, *adv.* = reasonably, 34.

Rebukede, 3*d sing. pf.* of rebuke, 32.

Reche, *v. tr.* = reach; 3*d sing. pres. ind.* recheth, 176; 3*d pl. pf.* rawʒten, 316.

Recke, *v. intr.* = reck, care; 3*d sing. pf. ind.* rowʒte, 177; 2*d sing. imper.* rekke, 306.

Rede, *v. tr.* = advise, 222; 1*st sing. pres. ind.* rede, 169.

Redresse, *v. tr.* 205.

Rekke. *See* Recke.

Rennen, *v. intr.* = run, 316 (?); *imp. pt.* rennynge, 113; 3*d pl. pf.* ronnen, 314, 321. *Rennene*, 316, may be *sb.* = rennenge *or* running, but is more likely the verb above.

Reredde, *p. pt.* of rere (rear); *v. tr.* 211.

Reste, *v. tr.* 77; 2*d sing. imper.* reste, 303.

Rewede, 3*d sing. pf. ind.* of rewe (rue); *v. tr.* = repent, be sorry for; used *impersonally*, 55; hym rewede = he was sorry.

Rewfulle, *adj.* 149.

Rewthe, *sb.* = ruth, sorrow, 102, 363.

Ring, *v. intr.*, 3*d pl. pf. ind.* rongen, 272.

Rongen. *See* Ring.

Rowte, *sb.* = crowd, 287.

Rowʒte. *See* Rekke, *v. intr.*

Ryche, *adj.* 271, 306, 363.

Rydethe, 3*d sing. pres. ind.* of ryde (ride); *v. intr.* 341; rydinge, *p. pt.* 228.

Ryuer, *sb.* 198; ryuere, 149, 350; *poss.* ryueres, 132.

Ryʒte, *adj.* = right, 222, 236, 336, 352; *sb.* 259; *pl.* 'his ryʒtes,' 283; *adv.* 32, 198, 205, 249.

Ryʒ[t]lye, *adv.* = rightly, 236.

Sadde, *adj.* 119. Perhaps = solid, massive (Cp. Wm. 1072); or else, and more probably = shed (O.E. *scaden*, from *scadan, v. tr.* Germ. *scheiden*). Cp. Gen. l. 58.

Sadelle, *sb.* 293.

Safe, *adj.* 43.

Same, *adj.* 34.

Saue, *v. tr.* 91; 3*d sing. pf. ind.* saued, 91.

Sauinge, *sb.* 194.

Sawe, *sb.* = that which is said, tale, 162, 253. *See also* Se, *v. tr.*

Sayde. *See* Seye.

Saye. *See* Se, *v. tr.*

Scharpelye, *adv.* 301.

Schreden, *v. tr.* = shred, 307.

Schyuered. *See* Shyuer.

Se, *v. tr.* = see, 359; 3*d sing. pres. ind.* seeth, 223; 1*st sing. pf.* saye, 5; seyʒe, 216; 3*d sing.* seyʒ, 22; syʒe, 202; sawe, 61, 340; 3*d sing. imper.* se, 26; used with *prep.*

of, 65 ; 1*st sing. pres. subj.* 74 ; *p. pl.* sene, 53.

Soche, *v. tr.* = seek ; *2d sing. imper.* seche, 53 ; *3d sing. pf. ind.* sowȝte, 60. Used intransitively in both places, in the sense of To betake oneself, go.

Seke, *v. tr.* = seek, 144.

Selfe, 73.

Selfen *or* Selven = self, and selves, 20, 47.

Seluer = silver, 43 ; seluere, 125.

Semelye, *adj.* = seemly, 42.

Sende, *v. tr.* 111 ; *3d sing. pres. ind.* sendethe, 88, 118 ; sendeth, 193 ; *3d sing. pf.* sente, 46, 129, 153.

Serue, *v. tr., intransitively* = be of use, 202 ; *3d sing. pres. ind.* seruethe, 218 ; *p. pt.* serued, 47 ;= deserve, *p. pt.* serued, 186 · seruethe, 194.

Seruyse, *sb.* = pay for service, 178.

Sethen. *See* Sythen.

Sette, *v. tr.* = set, 73.

Seueneth, *adj.* = seventh, 42.

Seuenne, *numeral adj.* = seven, 61.

Sex, *numeral adj.* = six, 42, 144, 347. *See also* Six.

Sexte, *adj.* = sixth, 160 ; sixte, 168, 369.

Seyde. *See* Seye, *v. tr.*

Seye, *v. tr.* = say, 74 ; sey, 213 ; *3d sing. ind. pres.* seyth, 252 ; seythe, 162, 245 ; *3d pl.* seyn, 217 ; *3d sing. pf.* sayde, 25 ; seyde, 28, 50, 64, 67-8, 77, 82, 127, 131, 177, 193, 197, 208, 213, 346, 349.

Seyȝ *and* Seyȝe. *See* Se, *v. tr.*

Shafte, *sb.* 301.

Shake, *v. tr.* *3d pl. pf. ind.* shoken, 356.

Shalle, *v.* *1st sing. pres. ind.* 75, 78, 139, 212, 239, 261, 288, 299, 330 ; *2d sing.* shalt, 54, 80, 238,

260 ; *3d sing. pf.* sholde, 94, 129, 202, 224, 282 ; shulde, 37, 96, 103, 191 ; *3d pl.* sholde, 12.

Shanke, *sb., pl.* shankes, 326.

She, *pers. pron.* 10, 26, &c.

Shelde, *sb.* = shield, 281, 298, 331.

Shene, *adj.* = shining, beautiful, 8 ; sheene, 298.

Shoken. *See* Shake, *v. tr.*

Sholde = should. *See* Shalle.

Sholder, *sb.* 222, 334.

Shrykede, *3d sing. pf. ind.* of shryke (shriek), 81.

Shulde = should. *See* Shalle.

Shylde, *v. tr.* = shield, 298.

Shyuer, *v. tr.* = smash, splinter ; *3d pl. pf. ind.* shyuereden, 315 ; *p. pt.* schyuered, 301.

Shyuereden. *See* Shyuer.

Six, *numeral adj.* 164, 193. *See* Sex.

Sixte, *adj.* = sixth, 369. *See also* Sexte.

Skape, *v. intr.* = escape, 127.

Sklawndered, *p. pt.* of sklawnder (slander) ; *v. tr.* = defame, accuse, 234.

Skorne, *sb.* 264.

Skylfully, *adv.* 47.

Slepte, *3d sing. pf. ind.* of sleep , *v. intr.* 192.

Slongen, *3d pl. pf. ind.* of sling ; *v. tr.* = to throw, 86 ; perhaps involving the idea of letting down by ropes ; as we *sling* horses in a transport-ship, or as we suspend an arm in a *sling.*

Slyppe, *v. intr.* = slip, 52.

Small, *adj.* 307, 330.

Smerte, *sb.* = smart, 308.

Smertlye, *adv.* = smartly, sharply, 318. It is miswritten *smerlye* in the MS.

Smyte, *v. tr.*, *3d sing. pf. ind.* smote, 146, 318; *3d pl.* smoten, 327; *2d sing. imper.* smyte, 311.

So, *adv.* 31, 70, 74, 103.

Sokour, *sb.* = succour, 111.

Somme, *adj.* = some, 111.

Sommene, *v. tr.* = summon, 187.

Sonde, *sb.* that which is sent, gift, 36.

Sone, *sb.* = son, 65, 78, 209, 347; sonne, 184, 211.

Soone, *adv.* 128, 208; sone, 105, 260-61.

Sorowefulle, *adj.* 91.

Sorwe, *sb.* = sorrow, 9; sorowe, 39, 78, 99, 359.

Sothe, *sb.* = truth, 18, 67, 131, 133, &c.

Sounde, *adj.* 43.

Sowke, *v. tr.* = suck, 115; *imp. pl.* sowkynge, 61.

Sowʒte. *See* Seche, *v.*

Speche, *sb.* 286.

Speke, *v. intr.* 249; *3d sing. pres. ind.* 252.

Spere, *sb.* = spear, 263, 315.

Spin, *v. intr.* = rush quickly; *3d sing. pres. indic.* spynnethe, 331. It is still used colloquially.

Spring, *v. intr.*, *3d sing. pf. ind.* spronge, 331.

Spronge. *See* Spring.

Spynnethe. *See* Spin.

Staffe, *sb.* 220.

Stalworth, *adj.* = stalwart, strong, 326.

Stand, *v. intr.*, *3d pl. pf. ind.* stoden, 147.

Stere, *v. intr.* = stir, move, 147.

Sterte, *v. intr.* = start; *3d pl. pres. indic.* sterten, 356; *3d pl. pf.* styrte, 326.

Steuenne, *sb.* = voice, 106, 149.

Stoden. *See* Stand.

Strawʒte. *See* Stretch.

Stretch, *v. intr.*, *3d pl. pf. ind.* strawʒte, 220.

Strike, *v. tr.*, *3d sing. pres. ind.* stryketh, 333; also *intransitively* = go; as we say, 'to strike across a field,' 229.

Stroke, *sb.* 333; *pl.* strokes, 298.

Stryketh. *See* Strike.

Styffe, *adj.* 241.

Styked, *3d sing. pf. ind.* of stick; *v. intr.* 241.

Stylle, *adj.* 147, 169.

Styrte. *See* Sterte.

Suche, *adj.* 202, 249, 264.

Sue, *v. tr.* = follow; *3d sing. pres. ind.* suwethe, 221; sueth, 230.

Sum, *adj.* = some, 57.

Swanne, *sb.* 148, 198, 350, 356, 358, 362.

Swerde, *sb.* = sword, 138, 146, 304, 306-7, 327-8.

Swete, *adj.* 44.

Sworn, *p. pt.* of swear; *v. tr.* 236.

Swyche, *adj.* = such, 49, 103, 139.

Swyde *for* Swythe, *adv.* = quickly, 158.

Swyfte, *adv.* 113.

Swymmen, *3d pl. pf. ind.* of swym (swim), 198, 350; *2d sing. pres.* swymmethe, 362.

Swyre, *sb.* = neck (O.E. *sweora*), 44, 126.

Syde, *sb.* 187.

Syken, *v. intr.* = to sigh; *3d sing. pres. ind.* syketh, 66; *3d sing. pf.* sykede, 25.

Syker, *adj.*, used *adverbially* = surely, 122.

Synne, *sb.* = sin, 250.

Sythen (Sithen) = since, then, 13, 25, 53, 64, 199; sethen, 116.

Sytte, *v. intr.* 22, 293.

Syȝe. *See* Se, *v. tr.*

Syȝte, *sb.* = sight, 122, 188.

Taber, *sb.* = tabor, 226.

Take, *v. tr.* = betake, commend, 104; also in its usual sense, 262; 2*d sing. imper.* 300; 3*d sing. pres. ind.* taketh, 116; takethe, 63, 150; 1*st sing. pf.* toke, 167; 2*d sing.* tokest, 237; 3*d sing.* toke, 159, 173, 229; 3*d pl.* 355; token, 226; *p. pt.* taken, 234.

Tale, *sb.* 55.

Tawȝte, *p. pt.* of teche (teach), 312, 336.

Telle, *v. tr.*, 1*st sing. pres. ind.* 162; 3*d sing.* tellethe, 7, 270; 3*d sing. pf.* tolde, 123, 347.

Tere, *sb.* = tear; *pl.* teres, 24.

Terme, *sb.* 140.

þanke, *sb.* = 194.

Thanke, *v. tr.*, 3*d sing. pf. ind.* thanked, 339; þankede, 36.

þanne, *adv.* = then, at that time, 73, 210.

þat, *art.* = the, 159, 296, 322, 366: *rel. pron.* 3, 4; *dem. pron.* 18, 27, &c.; by þat, 248, 345 = by that time; *conj.* 16, 26, &c.

The, *art.* 7, 11, 17, &c.

The, *pers. pron. obj.* = thee, 18, 65, 73, 77—79, 134, 139-40, 169, 184, 230, 237, 261, 311, 312, 336.

The, *pers. pron.* = they, 220, 274.

þeder, *adv.* = thither, 265.

Thefe, *sb.* 141, 199, 351.

Thei, *pers. pron. See* They.

Thenke, *v.* = think, 30, 249 (Cp. Wm. 4908); Germ. *denken;* 2*d sing. pf. ind.* thowȝte, 40, 207, 250, 264.

þenne, *conj.* = than, 125; *adv.* = when, 143; = at that time, 24,

41, 63, 67, &c.; ere thenne, 330 = before the time when; by thenne, 143 = by that time; = thence, 248.

þerby, *adv.* = near there, 265.

þere, *adv.* 13, 31, 87; = where, 76, 96, 121, 142, 362.

Therfore, *adv.* = on that account, 136.

þerin, *adv.* 52, 247.

þerof, *adv.* 115.

þerupon, *adv.* 282.

þese, *dem. pron. pl.* 93, 179, &c.

þey, *pers. pron. pl.* 12, 19, &c.; thei, 326. *See also* The.

This, *dem. pron.* 5, 92; er þis, 70 = before now.

Thoo, *adv.* = then, at that time, 339.

þorow, *prep.* = through, 95, 170.

þou, *pers. pron.* 50—54, &c.; thow, 80, 251.

þowghe, *conj.* = though, 100.

Thowȝte. *See* Thenke.

Thrydde, *adj.* = third, 367.

þus, *adv.* 89, 118.

þy, *poss. pron.* 65, 73.

Thykke, *adj.* = thick (closely covered), 294.

Thylle, *conj.* = till, 96.

Thynge, *sb.* 30, 202.

To, *prep.* 16, 17, &c.

Togedere, *adv.* = together, 20, 314; togedur, 327.

Toke
Token } *See* Take.

Topseyle, *adv.* = headlong, 320. *See* Note.

Towarde, *prep.* 33, 93, 109, 341.

Towre, *sb.* 280.

Trewe, *adj.* = true, 48, 69.

Trist, *v. tr.* = trust; 3*d sing. pf. ind.* triste, 49; truste, 285.

Trowthe, *sb.* = truth, 175.

Trumpe, *sb.* = trumpet, 226.

Truss, *v. tr.* to remove (Cotgrave, trousser, to trusse, tuck, packe, bind, or gird in, pluck, or twitch up); *3d sing. pres. ind.* trussethe, 327.

Truste, *v. tr. 3d sing. pf. ind.* 285.

Tryfulle, *v. intr.* = trifle, 48.

Tumbledde, *3d pl. pf. ind.* of tumble; *v. intr.* 320.

Turne, *sb.* in a good sense (as we say, 'to do one a good turn'), 139; in a bad sense, trick, wile, 257.

Turne, *v. tr., 3d sing. pres. ind.* turneth, 262; *3d sing. pf.* turned, 24, 341; *intr. 3d pres. ind.* 104, 150; *3d pl.* turnen. 355, 357; *3d sing. pf.* turnede, 123; *1st pl. imper.* turne, 93.

Twelfe, *numeral adj.* 243.

Tweyne, *numeral adj.* = two, twain, 29, 84.

Two, *numeral adj.* 23, 27, &c.; in two, 334.

Twynleng, *sb.* = a little twin, 27.

Tydynge, *sb.* 59; *pl.* tydynges, 58.

Tylle, *conj.* 310.

Tymber, *sb.* 317.

Tyme, *sb.* = time, 37, 55, 243.

Tyraunte, *sb.* = wicked, or evil man, 84. In Allit. the people of Sodom are called *tyrants*, B. 943.

Tyte, *adj.* = quick, 139. It is used here *adverbially*.

Tytlye, *adv.* = quickly, 84.

Unbounden, *p. pt.* of unbind; *v. tr.* 345.

Unbrente, *adj.* = unburnt, 185.

Under, *adv.* 21.

Undo = undone, *p. pt.* of undone, *v. tr.* = undo, 105.

Unsemelye, *adj.* 30.

Unto, *prep.* 90.

Unwerkethe, *adj.* = unworked, 175.

Up, *prep.* 64, 81, 97, &c.

Upon, *prep.* 19, 213, 222, 236, 281; = with, 361.

Valwe, *sb.* = value, 329.

Wakynge, *imp. pt.* of wake; *v. intr.* 207.

Walle, *sb.* 19, 349.

Ware, *adj.* 122.

Warne, *v. tr.* 190.

Was, *3d sing. pf. ind.* of be, 5, 6, &c.

Water, *sb.* 355, 362 = a piece of water, 51, 96.

We, *pers. pron. pl.* 3, 92, 302.

Wedde, *v. tr.* = bet, pledge, 27; *p. pt.* wedded = married, 69.

Wede, *sb.* = dress, clothing, 119; *pl.* wedes.

Wele, *adv.* = well, 2, 54, 67, 140, 309, 352; welle, 251.

Well, *v. intr.* = to bubble, pour forth copiously (O.E. *wellan* = to boil); *3d sing. pf. indic.* wellede, 166.

Welle, *adv.* 251.

Wende, *v. intr.* = go, 206; *3d sing. pres. indic.* wendes, 155, 178; wendethe, 161; wendeth, 190 (*see* Note); *3d pl. pres. indic.* wenden, 302, 364; *2d sing imper.* wende, 137.

Wene, *v. intr.* = ween, thinke (O.E. *wenan*); *1st sing pres. ind.* wene, 69; *3d sing. pf. indic.* wente, 67.

Wenten, *3d pl. pf. ind.*, serving as past tense of go; *v. intr.* 33; wente, 19; *3d sing. (reflexively* used) 75.

Were, *3d pl. pf. ind.* of be, 41, 58, 142; *3d sing. pf. subj.* 30, 67,

156; *3d pt.* 31; used for wast, *2d sing. pf. ind.* 237; *3d pl. pf. ind.* weren, 121.

Weren, *v. tr.* = defend (O.E. *werian;* Germ. *wehren*); *3d sing. pres. ind.* wereth, 2.

Werke, *sb.* = work, 2, 170, 330 (Germ. *werke*).

Werke, *v. tr.* = work, 78, 182 (O. Germ. *werken*).

Werue, *v. tr.* = deny, refuse (O.E. *wyrnau*), 56, 72.

Wesselle, *sb.* = vessel; or else silver plate. Fr. *vaisselle,* 156.

Wex, *v. intr.* = to wax, to grow; *3d sing. pres. indic.* wexeth, 158; *pf.* wexedde, 166.

Wey, *sb.* = way, 220.

Wey3te, *sb.* = weight, 155.

What, *rel. pron.* 56; *interrog.* 74.

Whelpe, *sb.* 61; welpe, 63.

Whenne, *adv.* = when, 1, 12, &c.

Where, *adv.* 12; *interrog.* 82.

Whyle, *adv.* 273; whyles, 145; whylle, 117; *sb.* 286.

Whyte, *adj.* 281.

With, *prep.* 2, 28, &c.; withe, 14, 23, &c.; wyth, 99.

Witty, *adj.* = cheerful (?), 35.

Wo, *sb.* 343.

Wolle, *v.*; *1st sing. pres. ind.* 244; *3d sing.* 252; *2d sing.* wolt, 72; *3d sing. pf. ind.* wolde, 30, 41, 56, 117, 164, 276. *See* Wylle.

Womman, *sb.* = woman, 22, 26, 38; *pl.* wymmen, 29.

Wondrethe, *3d sing. pres. ind.* of wonder; *v. intr.* 184.

Wonnen. *See* Wynne, *v. tr.*

Woode, *sb.* 113; wode, 119, 143, 215.

Worde, *sb.* 193, 207, 349; *pl.* worthes, 32.

Worlde, *sb.* 112, 180, 184.

Worse, *adj.* 244.

Worthes. *See* Word.

Wrake, *sb.* = punishment, 72. It is coupled with wrech = vengeauce, in Gen. 552.

Wrecche, *sb.* = wretch, 71.

Wrecched, *adj.* = wretched, 77.

Wronge, *sb.* 245; *adj.* used adverbially = wrongly, 170, 197, 349.

Wrow3te = wrought, *3d sing. pf. ind.* of work, 119.

Wryten, *p. pt.* of wryte; *v. tr.* 282.

Wyfe, *sb.* = wife, 69, 162, 169, 196.

Wylde, *adj.* 214.

Wyle, *sb.* = wile, 182.

Wylle, *sb.* = will, 1, 79, 181, &c.

Wylle, *v.*; *1st sing. pres. ind.* 128, 261; *2d sing.* 290; *2d sing.* wylt, 260. *See* Wolle.

Wynne, *v. tr.* = win; *p. pt.* wonnen, 170; *3d sing. pres. ind.* wynnethe = getteth, taketh, 337; thus miners speak of winning or getting out ores, or coals.

Wyse, *sb.* = wise, manner, 156.

Wyste. *See* Wytte.

Wyte, *v. tr.* = blame, 136.

Wytte, *v. tr.* = know; *2d sing. imper.* 195; *2d sing. pf. ind.* wysste, 35; *3d pl. pf.* wyste, 274; *2d sing. pf. subj.* 186.

Yen, *sb.* = eyen, eyne *or* eyes, 135, 323, 332.

Yf, *conj.* = if, 54.

Yle, *sb.* = isle, 5.

Yren, *sb.* = iron, 290.

3afe, *3d pl. pf. ind.* of give, 271.

3ate, *sb.* = gate, 22.

3e = yea, 212, 302.

3elde, *v. tr.* = yield, 335, 336. *See* Note.

49423

Ʒere, *sb.* = year, 89, 243.

Ʒonder, *adj.* (preceded by an article) = yonder, 26; ʒondur, 232; ʒondere, 233; *adv.* 198, 350.

Ʒonge, *adj.* = young, 81, 242, 251, 345.

Ʒosken, *v. intr.* = to hiccough, to sob; *3d pl. pf. ind.* ʒoskened, 108.

Ʒou, *pers. pron. obj.* = you, 100.

Ʒyf, *conj.* = if, 235.

Ʒyfte, *sb.* = gift, 271.

Ʒys = yes, 309.

RICHARD CLAY & SONS, LIMITED, LONDON & BUNGAY.